DRUID MAGE

Book 1 of the

C. S. Churton

Other Titles By C.S Churton

Druid Academy Series

DRUID MAGIC

FERAL MAGIC

TalentBorn Series

AWAKENING

EXILED

DEADLOCK

UNLEASHED

HUNTED

Available Soon

CHIMERA

Chapter One

I t was a beautiful day in a beautiful town – if you happened to like grey, overcast skies above even greyer streets. I didn't particularly care for either, but it was my town and today was going to be my day. I just knew it. I leaned back against the wooden bench and smiled, enjoying the little tingle of anticipation fluttering in my stomach as I looked at the white envelope in my hands.

A mewling sounded from somewhere around my feet, and I glanced down at the scruffy ginger tom cat.

"This?" I asked him, my grin spreading. "I'm glad you asked, kitty. *This* is, without a doubt, my university acceptance letter."

He mewled again, completely oblivious to my words, of course. My acceptance letter. It had to be. I just needed to actually open it.

The grey little town of Haleford wasn't renowned for its green spaces, but they were there, if you knew where to look. The one I'd come to today was little more than a handful of trees and a rustic wooden bench – and a cat, of course – and I took my time getting comfortable before I turned the envelope over in my hands. I'd applied for three universities and had in my possession two rejection letters. But this one was going to be different; I knew it. It wasn't as elite as Durham, nor as academic as London, but they had an excellent literature program, and it would be exactly the stepping stone I needed to launch myself into a career I could live with.

I ran my thumb under the flap and worked it loose. There was a single sheet inside, and with only the slightest tremble to my hands, I eased it from the envelope and carefully unfolded it. In the top right corner was emblazoned the Bristol University crest, and below it, a few typed lines. I ran my eyes over them.

Dear Ms Eldridge, Thank you for applying… Blah, blah, blah. *Bristol University receives thousands of requests…* Yada, yada. *We regret to inform you that on this occasion, we cannot offer you a place.*

Another rejection letter. That made it three for three. I leaned back against the bench with a sigh. There went my last chance of getting out of this dreary little town.

"I guess that's it for me," I said to the cat, forcing a blasé smile back onto my lips that didn't want to co-operate. "Time to resign myself to a lifetime of waiting tables."

The cat meowed loudly and swished its tail.

"Well, I'm not exactly thrilled either, Toby," I told the fleabitten animal. "But at least it means I'll be sticking around here to feed you."

Which was just as well, since I'd never seen another person nor animal in this spot. I folded my letter up with care it absolutely did not deserve, and pulled a wrapped sandwich and a bottle of water from my bag. It wasn't a particularly warm day, in fact it bordered on chilly, but I preferred not to go anywhere without some water. Besides, the sandwich had been in my bag for a while; it was probably a little dry by now. I set the bottle on the floor beside me and unwrapped the sandwich. I doubted the cat would care much for the wholemeal, so I slid the single slice of ham from between the bread and held it out. The tom snatched it from my hand and devoured it in seconds, then set about washing his paws. If only my life was so simple.

"A bit of food and you're happy. Where's your ambition?"

Probably wherever mine had disappeared to, and without weeks of tormenting himself, too. Maybe I should have been born a cat. I ate the rest of my lunch while he finished cleaning his paws and moved onto his face, watching me reproachfully the entire time.

I leaned back against the old wooden bench and unfolded the letter again, but if I'd been hoping it had reconsidered its hurtful words, I'd have been disappointed. Above me, the sky was darkening and the first drops of moisture were filling the air. Rain again – must be a 'y' in the day.

I reached down to scratch the tom absent-mindedly, my attention still on the printed words. From the corner of my eye I saw the first raindrop strike the animal right between his eyes. He hissed loudly, and slashed his claws at my hand.

"Ow!"

I yanked my hand away, but the damage was already done: four jagged red lines adorned my skin. Today just kept getting better and better. Movement caught my eye: a grey wisp spiralling up from my other hand. The letter! I released my grip on it, and the sheet fell to the floor, where it lay with an orange flame licking at one side of it. How the hell had it caught fire?

I broke out of my stupor and stamped on it, smothering the fire with my foot.

"What was that all about?" I asked the tom, plucking the letter from the floor and squinting at the still-smouldering corner. When I tore my eyes away from it, the cat was gone. Well, that figured. I shook my head and carefully folded up the remains of the letter and slid it back into its envelope. Just another day in paradise.

All things considered, I had bigger problems than disappearing cats and spontaneously combusting letters. A third rejection was bad news; worse was that I was going to have to break it to my parents. There was no way that conversation was going to end well. With a sigh, I thrust the envelope back into my bag, and headed for home.

*

"I'm sorry," I said, for the fourth time. I'd been counting.

"Sorry just isn't good enough, Lyssa," my dad was saying, standing rigid as he glared down at me, his eyes tight beneath his thick, grey brows. His words cut me more than his sharp tone, though that was pretty scathing, too. "This is your future we're talking about. You spent too much time with... with boys!"

"That's not fair!" No, really, it wasn't. Dillon wasn't even my boyfriend, and the hours I'd told my dad had been spent studying really had been spent studying. I folded my arms across my chest. "It's not my fault I'm not academically gifted. We can't all be like you and Holly."

"Don't bring your sister into this." For a moment he looked like he was going to really lose it, but my mum placed a hand on his arm.

"Come now, George, she tried her best. There are other things in life than just school."

"Just school? What sort of future will the girl have without an education?"

I tapped my foot on the tiled floor of our kitchen, earning me a glare from both my parents. Like I cared. Tap. Tap. Tap. Except I did care. About all of it. I wanted to be more like my dad and Holly. Someone my parents could be proud of. I didn't want to be a disappointment. I dropped my arms to my sides and stilled my foot.

"Mum, Dad, I really am—"

"Lyssa, you have nothing to apologise for," my mum interrupted, before fixing Dad with a stare. "Does she, George?"

He cleared his throat. A shade over six foot tall, and a highly successful lawyer, there were few things in life that intimidated my dad. My five-foot-nothing mum happened to be one of them.

"No, no I suppose not. She tried her best."

"I really did, Dad, I promise."

He exhaled slowly and nodded.

"I know you did. You can always resit your exams and apply again next year."

Oh, joy. That would be something to look forward to. I swallowed the groan rising up in my throat and just nodded.

"Of course, Dad. I'll do better next time."

I slunk out from beneath the weight of his disappointment and made a beeline for my room, dropping straight down onto my bed as soon as the door was shut behind me. I'd been lying back, staring up at the ceiling, picturing exactly how bleak the rest of my summer was about to become, when I recalled the letter in my bag. I swung my legs over the side of my bed and pulled it out, easing it from its envelope once again. There, in the bottom right corner – or rather, what remained of it – was a black smudge, smeared about the crisp black edge. Right where I'd been holding it. Weird.

I kept staring at it – why, I don't know. Maybe I was waiting for it to come to life and explain itself, which seemed about as likely as it catching fire in the first place. People had gone insane over lesser things than getting rejected for a school they hadn't truly wanted to go to in the first place. I blew air through my lips, then dumped the letter beside me on the bed and looked over at my immaculate desk, its top clear except for my laptop, and– Oh. That was odd. Another letter. Maybe my parents left it there? They must have forgotten to mention it in the big reveal of what an utter disappointment I was.

I hopped off the bed and picked up the stiff white envelope. Emblazoned on the front in elegant, flowing letters were the words *Lyssa Eldridge.*

Nothing else. No address, no stamp. Just my name. Huh. Odd. I turned it over and carefully unstuck the flap. Inside was a single sheet of equally stiff white parchment. I opened it up and smoothed it out, although the creases along the fold lines didn't seem nearly so deep as I'd expected. Maybe expensive paper didn't crease as much as the normal stuff.

At the top of the page was a crest unlike any I'd seen before. It didn't belong to any university I knew. In the centre was a tree that might have been an oak and beneath it to one side was a dragon, and facing it from the other, some sort of winged horse. Each quarter of the crest was a different colour – crimson red, bright blue, emerald green, and citrus yellow. The mix should have been jarring, but somehow it wasn't.

Dear Ms Eldridge, the letter began. *It is with great pleasure that I inform you that you have been accepted to study at the Dragondale Academy of Druidic Magic.*

Druidic magic? A strangled laugh slipped up from my throat and I looked around.

"Alright, Holly, very funny. You can come out now."

My little sister wasn't much of a prankster, she was usually much too serious for that, but when the mood took her, she didn't do things by halves. I had to admit, the unique crest and the expensive paper were nice touches. Excellent attention to detail.

"Come on, I know you're in here somewhere."

I listened for the telltale giggle, but there was only silence. A quick search around my modest-sized and sparsely decorated room soon revealed I was on my own.

Guess she got bored of waiting for me to get back and find her little surprise. I picked it up from the desk with a smile. It really was elegantly done. I scanned the rest of the letter and gave her extra credit for including the date term was due to start – although it was a full fortnight earlier than actual universities started – and details of how I was to reach the academy, via a portal in my local 'druid grove'. Very creative. And the signature at the bottom, a Professor Talendale, Headmaster of Dragondale, was so intricate it must have taken her forever to come up with, and as I held it up, it almost seemed to shimmer in the sunlight. I wondered what ink she'd used.

"You got the title wrong, Hols," I said under my breath, dropping the letter back onto my desk besides its envelope. "Universities don't have headmasters. And forgetting to put the address on the envelope? Amateurish."

I fired up my laptop and jumped onto my school's website. Might as well find out about resitting those exams. I heaved a sigh as I got started, and promptly forgot all about the strange letter.

Chapter Two

As predicted, my summer disappeared under a pile of books. I wasn't sure how many strings my dad had pulled to allow me to retake the entire year's classes, for which I was sure I'd one day find some way to repay him, but he seemed content that my future was secured, at least for the moment. I didn't want to find out what his reaction would be if I failed a second time, so I obligingly spent long summer days buried under an ever-growing pile of texts books, trying to appear grateful. At least once a day I would head back to my favourite clearing, with my favourite cranky old tom cat. Nothing else ever burst into flames.

It was on one of those days, as summer was drawing to an end, that I saw him. At first, I thought I must have spent too much time studying and my brain had taken a little time out, because no-one ever came to the clearing, and certainly no-one who looked quite like him. In fact, I didn't think I'd ever seen anyone who looked quite like he did. He was tall and scrawny, with a slicked back hair streaked with grey. He wore what appeared to be a cloak, bright yellow and trimmed with blue, with some sort of black robes underneath, and a pair of wire-rimmed glasses that seemed to be perpetually sliding down his nose.

Stranger still, as he stepped out from the bushes, he looked around, fixed his eyes on me, and stepped forward with a curt nod.

"Ah, good, you're here. And on time, too. Excellent. Talendale abhors tardiness."

He spoke with an upper-class twang, and it took me a moment to process his words.

"Um... excuse me?"

I glanced over my shoulder in case he was talking to someone behind me, but we were quite alone, other than Toby. The tom hopped to his feet and rubbed himself against the strange man's legs. *Traitor.* The best I'd ever managed with him was not being bitten.

"You are Lyssa Eldridge, correct?"

"Well, yeah, but–"

"And you did receive your letter, correct?"

"Yeah– Well, no, I mean– What letter?"

"Rather small, this druid grove, isn't it?" he said, squinting around the clearing as though seeing it for the first time. "Still, I suppose you are the only druid in Haleford."

"I'm sorry, this what grove? Wait, did you just call me a... a druid?"

He pushed his glasses up his nose and looked at me like I was the one who'd gone mad, which was rich.

"Well, of course you're a druid, what else would you be? And this—" he swept his arms, gesturing grandly to my humble little hideout, "is your druid grove, your protected space in which to practice magic. It's shielded from outside observers, and of course mundanes can't enter, though—"

"Mundanes?" I interrupted.

"Humans and creatures without magic – are you sure your mentor didn't tell you any of this?"

He peered at me over the top of his glasses with a frown.

"This really is all rather elementary."

"Uh-huh. I'm sure." This whole conversation was getting ridiculous. Shielded groves and druids and places non-magical creatures couldn't enter, and—

"What about him?"

I nodded to the cat that had stopped rubbing against the stranger's legs and had started washing his whiskers.

"Hm, Toby? What about him?"

"He's a cat, he's not a mag— Wait, how did you know his name's Toby?"

"He lives at the academy, when he's not wandering through the mortal realms. Everyone knows his name."

"Then, how do I know his name?"

The stranger's forehead creased, and I replayed the words through my head and tried to work out how to reword them so that they sounded less ridiculous. How exactly was it I was the one needing to explain themselves in this particular conversation?

"I mean, I've never been to this... academy, or whatever, so no-one could have told me. It's just what I've always called him."

"Oh, I see. Well, Toby isn't actually a cat, he's a wampus. This form is just the one he chooses to assume outside of the academy's grounds. Which is where he should be right now."

He raised an eyebrow at the cat – wampus – whatever, apparently completely oblivious to the fact that he had in no way answered my question, but had managed to raise at least a dozen more. Toby hissed at him, then darted into the bushes.

"Toby prefers not to portal in front of people."

"Uh-huh. Of course."

He was obviously crazy, and possibly not the harmless kind, so I figured going along with it all was probably the best option right now.

"Well, it's been lovely meeting you, Mr, uh–"

"Oh, where are my manners?" He looked startled at his oversight and hastily composed himself, pushing his glasses up his nose another time, and straightening the clasp on the front of his cloak.

"Rufus Oswald Hamilton Pembington the Fourteenth, recruiter for the Dragondale Academy of Druidic Magic, and assistant to Professor Talendale, at your service."

He folded one arm over his waist and gave a curt bow.

"Right. Well, Mr... Pembington, I really should be leaving now."

"Pardon me? Leaving? Oh no, I'm afraid that's quite impossible. We're already late, and the headmaster will be expecting you."

I frowned, replaying his words. Headmaster Talendale. Dragondale Academy of Druidic Magic. Those were all names from that letter Holly wrote me right after I got rejected from Bristol University. How did Rufus Osmond the whatever know about a hoax letter? I never showed it to anyone. I never even got around to talking to Holly about it. I took a breath.

I mean, what if... what if Holly didn't write the letter?

I laughed and shook my head. Dragondale Academy of Druidic Magic? Of course it wasn't real.

"Something amusing you, Ms Eldridge?"

"Yeah, look, no offence Mr Pemberton–"

"–Pembington."

"–But I'm not going to any academy."

"All juvenile druids are required by law to attend the academy of their patriarchal line. And if we don't leave immediately, we are going to be late. Professor Talendale abhors–"

"Tardiness. Yeah, you said. There's no way I'm getting into a car with you."

"A car? One of those mundane contraptions? Certainly not. We shall travel by portal."

"Por–" Whatever smart mouthed reply I'd been about to deliver was cut off by the sudden appearance of what could only be a portal. One moment I was staring at a patch of grass in front of a wilting bush, and the next there was an image of what I could only describe as a castle set behind iron wrought gates, floating in the air in front of me.

"What is that?"

"That," Rufus said grandly, "is the Dragondale Academy of Druidic Magic."

"No, I mean," I gestured to the floating patch of colour, "What's that?"

"Why, that's a portal, of course. Surely you've seen a portal before?"

His brow furrowed in concern that would have been condescending if it wasn't all so bizarre. I ignored him and peered cautiously round the back of the portal, where the rest of my little clearing was exactly as it always had been. It was as if someone had suspended a movie screen in mid-air. I stretched a hand out towards the image on its front.

"I wouldn't do that if I were you," Rufus said, clearing his throat. "You wouldn't want one part of you to be here and the other in the academy now, would you, hm?"

No, probably not. I dropped my hand back to my side.

"It's all real? The portal, the academy... magic?"

"Are you always this slow on the update, Ms Eldridge? Professor Talendale won't be happy."

"Well, excuse me if this is all a bit of a shock," I snapped, putting my hands on my hips and then immediately feeling like an idiot.

"You *did* receive your letter," Rufus reminded me.

"Yes, I know I received the letter, but—" I cut off with a groan of frustration. This bizarre conversation was going round in circles, and frankly I wasn't convinced that stepping into a floating movie screen was going to do anything other than give me a bruise on my face. I looked at it again. The castle – or academy, I supposed – was easily bigger than any building I'd ever been in, maybe bigger than any I'd ever seen. It was made of chiselled grey stones and what looked to be stained glass windows, and it had several towers at either end. It was set in an endless expanse of green, with a backdrop of the brightest blue sky, and flying around one of the towers was…

"Is that a dragon?"

"Hm?" Rufus peered into the portal. "Ah, yes, they must be exercising Paethio. Don't fear, he's quite tame. It's Dardyr you need to watch out for."

"There are… dragons?"

"Why, of course. You could hardly have the *Dragondale* Academy of Druidic Magic without dragons now, could you, hm?"

Dragons. Right. I was staring at a portal to a magic academy that had *dragons*. If you'd said that the king of rock and roll had stepped out of his grave and popped by for a cup of tea, I don't think I could have been any more surprised.

"Come now, we mustn't linger. The whole school's schedule will be disrupted if we're late, and Professor Talendale wouldn't like that at all. Not at all."

"Right. Can't keep Professor Talendale waiting."

"Quite," Rufus agreed with a sage nod, as if he hadn't noticed the sarcasm in my voice. "After you, Ms Eldridge. Simply step through."

Nothing about the idea of stepping through a magic portal sounded simple to me, but I stepped closer to it anyway, and tried to line myself up – because I didn't want to leave a bit of me behind. I sucked in a deep breath, exhaled it slowly, and then stepped into the portal.

I made it to the far side with all of my fingers and toes, and no small amount of relief. I looked around me and burst out laughing.

"Is something else amusing you, Ms Eldridge?" Rufus asked, stepping from the portal behind me and looking mildly irked – although given that all his emotions appeared mild, he could have been absolutely fuming for all I knew. I made an effort to stifle my laughter.

"I'm sorry, it's just… it's all so ridiculous."

And it was. I wasn't standing in my clearing in Haleford anymore. I was standing outside the gates of the building I'd seen in the floating movie screen – the floating movie screen I'd somehow walked through – and any time soon I was going to wake up in my own bed and laugh about this whole ridiculous dream.

"There is nothing ridiculous about the Dragondale Academy of Druidic Magic," Rufus hmphed.

"No, I didn't mean…" I trailed off, peering through the gates at the vast castle. It was even bigger than it had appeared through the portal. "This place is incredible."

Rufus seemed placated by my obvious awe, and smiled with a touch of smugness.

"Rather. It is quite something to behold. Over fifty thousand druids have studied in our ancient halls. The

Dragondale Academy of Druidic Magic is a noble institution, steeped in honour and tradition."

"Student name?" The voice came from what appeared to be a solid wall beside the gate, but as I looked closer I saw a hatch in the brickwork at about knee-height. Through the small window, a pair of yellowish eyes stared at me.

"Um… Uh… Lyssa Eldridge," I managed after a moment.

The eyes disappeared and I fidgeted, staring at the hatch and wondering what very short creature with yellow eyes was concealed inside it.

"Goblin," Rufus whispered from the corner of his mouth. "Excellent gate guardians, not to be trifled with."

"Lyssa Eldridge," the goblin said, making me jump and sounding like the words left a bad taste in his mouth. "You're late."

"I'm sorry, I didn't know," I tried to explain, but the eyes had vanished again.

"Why did he say my name like that?" I whispered to Rufus.

"Hm? Oh, try not to pay attention to that."

I was about to press him for more answers when the gates swung inwards with a creak.

I took a hesitant step through, wondering what on earth had happened to my nice, normal life. Rufus swept his arm towards the huge oak doors and smiled broadly.

"Welcome to the Dragondale Academy of Druidic Magic."

Chapter Three

Rufus wasted no time leading me up to the giant oaken doors, which opened seemingly by themselves at our approach. I shot Rufus a look, waiting for him to tell me there were more goblins here.

"The doors are enchanted. They open when they detect a magical creature approaching. One of the many safeguards against mundanes entering our hallowed halls."

Magic-detecting doors. Yeah, that wasn't weird. I hurried through, hoping the enchantment wouldn't wear off and cause them to squish me, but it wasn't until we were over the threshold that they started to swing closed. I spun in a circle, taking in the ceiling high above my head, and the banners hanging from the walls, interspersed between cabinets groaning with trophies and photos of previous students, going back what must have been hundreds of years. What on earth sort of competitions did druids get up to in their spare time? *Our* spare time, I supposed. I was a druid. I frowned and swayed a little on my feet as it started to sink in. I was a druid. I had magic and I'd come to a magical academy to be trained. Surreal didn't even begin to cover it.

"Quickly, please, Ms Eldridge. There will be plenty of time for sight-seeing later."

Right. We were late. I hurried to catch up with Rufus, because the last thing I wanted was to be lost in these vast corridors by myself. I'd never had a particularly good sense of direction at the best of times, and I was definitely not at my best right now. I took in as much as I could while keeping up with Rufus's long strides, looking left, right, up, and down, and trying not to trip over my own feet. High up in the corners, and along the length of the corridors were flaming torches that cast bright light in every direction as they flickered. I stopped for a moment and stared. They weren't torches. They were more like... like floating balls of fire.

"We really must be going straight to the main hall. I'll have someone take your bags to your–"

He broke off with a frown.

"Is that all the luggage you have, Ms Eldridge? Where are your books, your uniform, your ceremonial robes?"

All the 'luggage' I had with me was my backpack, filled with a couple of textbooks I'd been planning to revise from in the clearing, a bottle of water and a notepad.

"Well, I wasn't exactly expecting to come," I pointed out, trying not to sound snarky. "Wait, did you say uniform?"

"No matter," he said, hastening me along. "You can portal to the magical market this afternoon and get what supplies you require. Quickly now, this way, please."

He swung open a door before I could ask how I was supposed to know where to go, or what supplies I needed, or even how I was going to pay for them – because I had a grand total of about a fiver in my pocket.

My questions died on my lips as I peered in through the door at the huge room, with more of the fireballs floating by the ceiling. I wondered for a moment how the whole place didn't catch fire, but the flames never touched a thing, just flickered contentedly mid-air. Which was just as well, since all the furniture in the room was wooden, and the stone walls were draped with more banners and tapestries, these ones depicting people in cloaks, alongsside dragons and flying horses, and a whole menagerie of other creatures I didn't recognise. The itself room was a designer's fantasy, oozing with seventeenth century charm – high ceilings, exposed beams that twisted like living branches, and arched doorways. The cobbled floor was lined with chairs – at least a several hundred of them – all facing a stage. Most of the chairs were already occupied, so when Rufus gave me what I'm sure was supposed to be an encouraging nudge, I stumbled into the hall, almost falling over my own feet in the process, and sunk into the nearest unoccupied seat.

The girl in the seat beside me turned to me with a wide smile, revealing a set of perfect teeth that seemed to glisten under the flickering fireballs. Her green eyes seemed to sparkle with excitement – trick of the light, I'm sure.

"Are you a first year, too?" she whispered, pushing a lock of her straight reddish hair from her pale face.

"Um, yeah, I guess."

"I'm so excited to finally be here," she gushed. "I've heard so much about it."

"From who?"

She gave me a funny look.

"Why, from my parents, of course." She gasped and her hand flew up to her pink lips. "Are you the firstgen?"

"The first what?"

"The firstgen – a first generation druid. You know, the first one in your family? I heard there was a firstgen starting this year. There hasn't been one in over fifty years."

"I... I suppose so?" It came out more like a question. I mean, I'd never seen either of my parents throwing around magic, and no-one had told *me* about the academy, and you'd have to think this was the sort of thing they'd have mentioned. And why else would they have been so obsessed about my university rejection letters, and insist I study to resit my exams? No, they couldn't have known anything about this, not–

"Oh my God, my parents!"

"What about them?"

For a second I forgot the girl sitting there, caught up as I was in my horrifying realisation. The words poured out of my mouth, leaving me with an empty, queasy feeling.

"They don't know I've come here. They'll be expecting me home in a couple of hours."

"Oh no!" The girl's forehead furrowed for a moment, and then she brightened. "I bet the headmaster will let you contact them if you explain. Everyone's very nice here, or so I've heard. I'll help you find his office later. I have the academy map memorised."

"Uh, thanks."

"No problem. I'm Kelsey Winters, by the way."

"Lyssa Eldridge."

I shook her hand but was prevented from saying anything else by the figure who stepped onto the stage. A hush fell over the entire room. The man was wearing a long, heavy robe swirled with red, blue, yellow and green that reached right to the floor and trailed slightly behind him. He looked to be in his fifties, with short, dark hair and wrinkles starting to set into his face, which wore a stern expression as he looked out over the sea of students.

"Greetings, students, and welcome to the Dragondale Academy of Druidic Magic, or welcome back to our second and third years. For those of you who do not know, I am Professor Talendale and I am your headmaster. Alongside the other professors, I will be over-seeing your education in the coming year, and I expect you all to give your absolute best in every lesson you attend."

He swept that imperious gaze over us all, and I shrank further into my seat. Just great. There was a reason I hadn't been able to get a place at any of the universities I'd applied to. All I needed was another set of lessons to fail.

"Firstly, to address the rumours you may have heard that we have a first generation druid joining us this year, I can confirm that this is correct. I hope you will all make Ms Avery feel very welcome here."

Ms Avery? My mouth popped open and I felt rather than saw the sideways glance Kelsey gave me. Who the hell was Ms Avery? And did that mean one of my parents was a druid? No, surely not. Not my parents – they were as ordinary and mundane as it was possible to be. There must have been some sort of mistake, that was all. Two firstgens after none in fifty years, though. What were the odds?

"Now, as I'm sure you are all aware, you will be sorted according to your primary element. The four elemental houses are Earth, Air, Fire and Water. Heads of Elements, please make yourselves known."

Four figures seated near the front stood up and turned around to face us. They each wore a robe – one emerald green, one citrus yellow, one crimson red and the other brilliant blue. They waved, and then took their seats again.

"Your dormitories will be assigned by element, and I urge you to bring honour to your house. Those of you who do not yet know your primary element, you may find your name on your elemental house list, posted at the rear of the hall."

A few necks craned backwards, staring at the wall behind me. I tried not to make accidental eye contact with anyone, and stared at my feet until the headmaster spoke again.

"Is there a Lyssa Eldridge in the hall?"

A murmuring started up, and Kelsey stared at me with her mouth hanging open.

"Stand up," she hissed from the corner of her mouth, her eyes almost as wide as mine. I scraped my chair back and stood on unsteady legs, cringing and trying to ignore the hundreds of pairs of eyes staring at me with unhidden curiosity. The silence was absolute.

"Ah, Ms Eldridge, good. There was some dispute regarding to which elemental house you belong, given your... unique situation."

Unique situation? What unique situation? I said nothing, just turned steadily redder as I tried not to look at anyone.

"You will present yourself in my office later this morning, so that we may discuss where you are to be placed."

He continued to stare at me. I gave a shaky nod, not really sure how else I should react, and not trusting my voice with all the other students staring at me.

"Very well, you may be seated."

I sunk back into my chair and the students all faced forwards again – all except for Kelsey, who was still staring at me with wide eyes and mouth agape. I gave her my best 'don't ask me' shrug and avoided her eye.

"Finally," Professor Talendale continued, "A reminder that the academy grounds are off limits to first years after dark. Further, the Unhallowed Grove is also off limits to all students this year. Failure to observe this rule will result in detention, or in extreme cases, expulsion."

Detention? I held back a snort. For a moment I felt like I was back in high school. No-one else seemed to find it amusing though, so I kept my thoughts to myself. The professor looked around the hall with hooded eyes for a long moment, and then gave a curt nod.

"Classes will begin tomorrow. You may spend the rest of the day getting acclimated, and should you have any questions, your elemental heads will be able to assist you. You are dismissed."

Chapter Four

The din of several hundred people leaving the hall was so loud that I had to lean close to Kelsey as we left the hall so she could hear what I was saying.

"You don't need to check your Elemental whatever assignment?" I practically shouted, as we passed a small group of first years clustered round the lists pinned on the wall. Kelsey shook her head, sending thick red locks cascading around her face.

"Elemental House. And no, my elemental power already manifested itself. I'm a Fire."

"Oh. Cool."

I nodded and try to look as if it meant something to me, but I had no idea if any of the houses were better than the others, or if being in Fire was a good thing. I followed her lead as she strode through the corridors like she'd been here all her life.

"My father is a Fire," she said, "So it was always likely that I would be, too. Speaking of which, I thought you said you were a newgen?"

"I thought I was. I mean, I am. It must have been some sort of mistake."

She looked at me like I was crazy and tucked her head down as we walked.

"Alright, what?" I asked eventually. "What am I missing?"

"Well, the admission letters are sent out by the Tilimeuse Tree in the centre of the academy's grounds. It knows every druid who is the son or daughter of a former Dragondale student, and every newgen born in all of England. The Tilimeuse Tree is as old as the academy itself. It doesn't make mistakes."

"The lineage thing, it's patriarchal, right?" At least, I was pretty sure that's what Rufus had said back in the clearing-grove-thingy, although it was all a little blurry. My head was swimming with all the new information crammed inside it. "Which means my dad would have to have been a druid. And trust me, there is absolutely no way he knows anything about magic."

The thought of my father, the lawyer, who placed a premium on everything being correct and orderly, whipping out a magic wand was frankly laughable.

"Hm, well, it would be odd of him to have kept it from you, and not told you about any of this," Kelsey said, her brow knitting. "But the tree has never made a single mistake in the entire history of Dragondale."

"I don't know what to tell you. I guess I'm just the odd one out."

"You're not wrong about that," Kelsey said, steering us round a corner and up a steep flight of stairs – the fourth, if I'd kept count correctly. "I've never heard of Professor Talendale summoning a first year into his office. Not before they've had a chance to get into trouble, anyway."

She looked at me askance, as though she was suddenly worried about being seen with me, and ventured,

"You're not a troublemaker, are you?"

"Not usually."

"Good. You do know what happens to druids who are expelled, don't you?"

I sighed with what little breath I had left by the time we'd crested the stone stairs.

"Kelsey, I hadn't even heard of Dragondale this morning. How do you think I could possibly know the answer to that?"

"Their magic gets bound." She stared at me, and when I apparently didn't look horrified enough, she clarified, "Stripped! Your magic gets stripped and you have to live like a mundane."

"Terrible," I said, with mock horror, though my new friend didn't pick up on the mock part.

"Yes, it would be," she said with a shudder. "I can't think of anything worse."

I stared at her in disbelief for a long moment, deliberating on whether she was completely insane, or if she'd just led a very sheltered life, before I realised we'd stopped walking. We were standing in front of a huge wooden door, which reached halfway to the high ceiling, and was wide enough for four people to enter abreast. The metal hinges were almost the width of my hand, and I could see no visible handle.

"This is it," she said. "Professor Talendale's office. I'd best be going. It was nice meeting you, Lyssa.

"You too, Kelsey."

I raised my hand and knocked once on the door. From within, a voice boomed.

"Come."

I looked again at the heavy door with no handle and wondered exactly how I was supposed to do that. I was just about to try giving it a shove when it swung inwards of its own volition.

I ventured one foot through the threshold, then hurried the rest of me across lest it swung shut while I was in its way. Doorways were definitely going to be a problem for me here. It might help if they weren't all triple the size of normal doors and made of enough heavy wood to crush me if they decided I wasn't magical.

The room was expansive and elegantly furnished, with woven rugs covering some of the stone floor, and the remaining exposed stones were immaculately clean and smooth. Banners hung from the walls: one elemental colour on each side, and in between them were dozens of bookcases, packed with volumes whose names I couldn't read from here.

In the centre of the room was a large desk made of pale wood, etched with hundreds of intricate carvings. My eyes didn't linger long, because the man behind the desk rose to his feet, commanding my attention. He was no less impressive up close, nor any less intimidating.

"Ms Eldridge," Professor Talendale said. "Thank you for coming. I appreciate your punctuality."

He waved a hand, and a creak sounded from behind me. I spun round in time to see the door ease back into its frame, and a shimmer of green light pass over it and then vanish.

"Please, take a seat," the headmaster said, gesturing to one of several chairs positioned in front of his desk, carved with the same designs as the monstrous desk itself. I sank into one, feeling like... well, like a kid who'd been summoned to meet the headmaster, I suppose. The fact that these chairs were clearly designed for someone several feet taller than me wasn't helping. I perched an elbow on the chair's armrest and tried to find an angle that was comfortable.

The headmaster didn't take his seat. Instead, he clasped his hands behind his back and started to pace.

"Yours is a most unusual case, Ms Eldridge. As you may know, the Tree of Tilimeuse detects those druids who belong here at Dragondale, as well as their primary element. In your case, it seems it was unable to do the latter."

He frowned deeply, like that was somehow my fault, which I thought was a bit harsh, considering I'd never even seen the Tree of Tilimeuse. I meant to nod and keep a serious expression, but what I actually did was open my mouth and let the first thought that came to mind escape.

"It was mistaken about me there only being one newgen, too, sir."

He stopped mid-stride and glared at me.

"The Tree of Tilimeuse is not mistaken. It does not make mistakes."

"But–" I almost lost my nerve then, with those pale green eyes boring into me. I swallowed my cowardice. "But my dad isn't a druid, sir. Nor... Nor's my mum. I mean, they can't be, they've never done magic before."

I was dangerously close to blabbering, so I clamped my jaw shut. Meanwhile, Professor Talendale's eyebrows shot right up.

"Not magical, you say?" he muttered. "Impossible, impossible. Unless..."

He placed a palm flat onto his desk, and the carvings started to crawl across the wooden surface, like snakes through grass. I stared in equal parts fascination and horror, until I felt a prickling sensation on my skin and looked down at my chair. The engravings on my seat had started moving, too. I leapt out of it, almost knocking it over in the process, and scratched furiously at myself.

"How are they doing that?" I stammered.

"Hush, hush," the headmaster said, still staring at his desktop and the newly-formed patterns on its surface. He glanced up at me through his brows. "Sit back down. It's perfectly harmless."

I wasn't convinced about that, but Professor Talendale's tone left no room for discussion, so I crept back towards the chair, and perched on its very edge, touching as little of it as possible, and kept one eye on the roving etchings. At least none of them were trying to move from the chair onto me. In fact, now that I'd finished panicking, it was kind of fascinating. I stretched out a tentative hand and prodded a bit of wood that'd had an etching on it just moments ago, before it had slithered away. It was perfectly smooth, like it had never been engraved. How peculiar. I wondered what would happen if I held my finger in the path of one of the engravings, and was just psyching myself up to do that when the professor spoke.

"Ah, most interesting."

I pulled my hand back and looked across the desk at him. He was still gazing at its surface. Some of his engravings had arranged themselves into pictures and words. I craned my neck for a look but couldn't quite make them out.

"Interesting, indeed." He rubbed his chin and continued to stare at the desktop, until my nerves felt like they might snap.

"What's interesting?" The words burst out of my mouth without permission for the second time in a matter of minutes. This time I gave a mental shrug and let it go.

"Your biological parents have magic, or at least, your biological mother–"

"What do you mean, biological?"

The professor looked irked by my interruption, but I didn't much care at that moment, because I'd only ever heard parents referred to as 'biological' in one context.

"Why, the parents who gave birth to you, of course, not those who raised you."

"What are you talking about?" I was on my feet again without meaning to be, my hands curled into fists by my sides.

"You're adopted. Did you not know?"

"I'm supposed to believe that, just because some carvings say so?"

"Hm?" He followed the direction of my eyes, which were fixed on the desktop. I had a much better perspective to read from, now I was on my feet. "Oh, there aren't carvings. This desk is formed from wood harvested from the Tilimeuse Tree. The messages you see come directly from the tree itself."

"Well, it's wrong then!"

"Ms Eldridge, control your temper. I understand this may have come as a bit of a shock to you–"

Now that was the understatement of the century… but, well, it couldn't be true. It just couldn't. Could it?

"–but you will conduct yourself with respect inside this academy, if you wish to remain a student here."

I swallowed both my anger, and my pride. I didn't want to get kicked out on my first day. Besides, if what he was saying *was* true, how else would I find out about my real parents? Or biological ones, whatever.

"I apologise, Professor."

"Hm? That's quite okay, dear."

The professor's mercurial moods were making me dizzy. His attention was back on the desk again. His thick eyebrows were knitted together.

"I've never seen anything quite like it," he muttered to himself. "No wonder there was some confusion…"

"Uh, Professor?"

"Oh. Yes. You see, the tree keeps detailed records of the lineage of every druid who attends Dragondale. Yet here– The tree seems to have no record of who your father is, nor anyone on your paternal side."

"How is that possible?"

"I don't know." He stroked his chin again. "He was almost certainly a former student here at Dragondale, otherwise the tree would not have summoned you to attend, yet there is no record of him. I've never seen this before."

He coughed and waved his hand over the desk. The etchings dispersed and then stopped moving.

"No matter. That's not what we are here to discuss."

"It's not?"

"No. The tree was unable to determine your primary elemental power. It has been fluctuating between water and fire since the moment it revealed your name. Now, Lyssa, an elemental druid can manifest more than one element, though usually not until much later in their studies, and never an element opposite to their primary, therefore you cannot possibly possess both water and fire powers. Have you any idea which element your powers favour?"

He'd been leaning further and further forward during his speech, until he was looming halfway over the desk and staring into my face.

"Um…"

How on earth was I supposed to know? I didn't know a thing about any of this until earlier today. And I'd certainly never shown any sign of magic powers. Nothing even remotely weird had ever happened to me. Except…

"A few weeks ago, I was holding a letter, and one corner kind of… caught fire? I'm not sure how it happened."

The professor nodded sagely.

"Then it's settled. You are a fire element. Very good. I suspected as much from your fiery nature. You may return to your dormitory; a bed will be assigned to you by the time you reach it."

"Um, Professor?"

I figured I might as well keep pushing my luck, while I was on a roll.

"My parents… I mean–" Well, they were still my parents, even if we weren't biologically related. Family is more than just blood. "They don't know I'm here. I didn't really know anything about it until Rufus turned up."

"Don't know that you're here? Goodness, girl, you must call them immediately. Though," he broke off and stroked his chin again, a habitual gesture that made me wonder if he'd recently shaved off a beard, "No, you mustn't reveal the true nature of our academy to mundanes to whom you are not related. Tell them where you are, but do not reveal the subject of your learning."

Well, that should be simple enough, since I hadn't learned anything yet, aside from the fact I might be adopted – and I was absolutely *not* having that conversation with the professor listening. I wasn't even sure I believed it.

Talendale handed me a phone which seemed completely out of place on the campus of a magical academy, and in an office which housed a desk made of magical wood capable to communicating with an ancient tree. The small black device seemed too mundane to belong in these settings. I could hardly picture all the students walking around in heavy robes, casting magic with one hand and holding mobile phones in the other.

"It is the only phone that works within the academy grounds," the professor said, as if reading my mind. "Though it is not powered by electricity."

I dialled the number and waited for the line to connect.

"Hello?"

I breathed a sigh of relief when I heard my mum's voice. This conversation would have been way too hard to have with my dad – it was virtually impossible to get anything past him. The lawyer in him could sniff out a half-truth a mile away.

"Hi, mum, it's me. Lyssa."

"Lyssa, I tried to call you. What time are you home?

"Yeah, that's the thing," I said, watching the professor from the corner of my eye. "Good news – I got accepted into a university out of town."

"Lyssa, that's wonderful! But isn't that a little short notice? Term must be starting in the next week or two."

I could practically hear her counting out the calendar in her head, and pressed on before she could work out the discrepancy.

"It starts tomorrow. I'm already here. There was a mix up with my acceptance letter."

"Your father will be thrilled. Wait... Don't you need you stuff? Your clothes and your books?"

"I can get everything I need here. Listen, I need to get everything sorted ready for tomorrow. I'll speak to you soon, okay?"

We said our goodbyes before I could blab anything about druids, or about them not being my birth parents, then I thanked the headmaster and made my escape from his office before I could say anything to him I shouldn't, either.

I found my way through the academy's ancient and maze-like hallways in a daze as I headed to the Fire dorms.

I couldn't believe it. I was a druid. The professors were going to teach me how to use magic. And I couldn't wait to get started.

Chapter Five

I reached the fire common room after only a small amount of getting lost – three wrong turns, and two helpful guides setting me back on course – and waited for the massive oak door to open itself. After a moment, I realised that wasn't going to happen.

"Oh." I grinned to myself, feeling like an idiot and giving it a shove. It was just an ordinary door.

A *locked* door. It refused to budge, even when I leaned my weight on it, just to be sure.

"You must be a first year."

I glanced back over my shoulder and saw a tall, heavy set guy in a red cloak watching me with a friendly smile on his face, and amusement crinkling the edges of his eyes.

"What gave it away?" I asked, returning his smile and gesturing my completely ordinary clothes with one hand.

"I take it you missed Dan's little chat with all the first years?"

"I guess so... is there some sort of password?"

"Sure is. Watch."

He leaned past me and planted his hand firmly on the door. I was just about to make some sort of sarcastic remark about how well that had worked for me, when my jaw popped open and refused to close again. As I watched, his palm gave a bright red pulse directly into the wood for a long second, and then three shorter pulses, then two more long ones. Was he… was he using magic? *Fire* magic?

"Whoa."

He removed his hand and the door swung open. He made a sweeping bow and gestured me inside, then followed behind me. As soon as we'd both crossed the threshold, the door swung shut with a dull thud.

"See you around, new girl."

He cut his way through the hoard of students easily, leaving me standing by the door, looking around in amazement. The room was huge and yet homely at the same time, with dozens of sofas and armchairs scattered around. Red rugs and banners decorated the stone floors and walls and as I looked more closely, I could see what looked like vines or twigs woven through the stones, leaving a trail of natural brown through the grey. More traces of the Tilimeuse Tree?

Fireballs hung suspended by the ceilings all around the room, so that even if large windows hadn't been set into each wall, there still would have been plenty of light. Each wall also had a large fireplace filled with yellow flames, and around one of them was a small gathering of students. One of the students – a girl with freckles and frizzy brown hair pulled back into a ponytail – was holding out her hand, and the flames changed size and shape seemingly at her command. They went from a homely fire to a roaring blaze that seemed as though it would set the entire room alight – yet somehow didn't – then right down to embers in a split second. Then flames erupted again, taking on the shape of a horse. I squinted as it sprouted wings and leapt from the fireplace then raced round the entire room, dodging the fireballs as it soared to the ceiling, and narrowly avoiding students' heads as it ducked low through the crowd.

The girl clenched her fist and the horse vanished as if it had never been there, the flames extinguishing themselves. Around her, the small circle of students clapped and cheered.

Insane. This whole place was insane. And incredible. My face split into a wide grin and I turned around – and almost walked straight into the girl from earlier. Kelsey.

"Lyssa, hi!" She smiled and stepped aside, her eyes glistening with excitement that spilled over into her rapid tones. "So, Professor Talendale placed you in Fire? That's great news. Do you know which room you're assigned to yet? There's an empty bed in my room, I bet that one's yours! I hope it is."

She clamped her hand over her mouth, and her face fell.

"I'm sorry, I'm talking too much again, aren't I? I always talk too much when I'm nervous, everyone says so. You can tell me to shut up. I don't mind."

I just chuckled.

"It's fine. You're fine. In fact, you're great."

She gave me a puzzled look.

"I am?"

"Yes, you are. You're the most normal person I've met since I got here."

"Oh." Her face fell again and she scuffed her feet, not meeting my eye. "You won't think that when you get to know about me. If you want normal, then you should make some other friends."

"Don't be silly," I said, slipping my arm through hers. "We're going to be great friends, I can tell."

"We are?"

"We are. Besides, how am I going to find my way around without you? This place is a maze."

"It is rather easy to get lost," she agreed with a chuckle. "Oh, that reminds me! We need to get you to the magical market so you can buy your uniform and books."

My thoughts went back to the handful of coins in my pocket. I didn't think they were going to buy me very much, and books were expensive.

"What's wrong?"

Kelsey was watching me closely, her face creased with concern.

"I, uh, I don't have any money. Not with me, anyway, at least not much. Not enough for books and uniforms."

"Oh, don't worry about that. The academy gives each student a small stipend at the start of the year. It's not much, but it should cover all the equipment you need. And you can get a job here on campus to earn anything else you need."

"Seriously? That's brilliant news. In that case, let's go shopping."

Getting to the market, unsurprisingly, meant using another portal. This one was set into a wall near the main hall, shaped like a doorway, and was entirely less unsettling that my first experience of portals had been. A prefect stood in front of it wearing heavy blue robes, stopping each student before they were allowed through. A strange black and gold bird was perched on his shoulder, and occasionally bent its head towards his ear like it was speaking to him. Both bird and prefect looked me and Kelsey up and down when we reached them.

"Names?" the prefect asked in a bored tone.

"Kelsey Winters and Lyssa Eldridge," Kelsey answered quickly.

The bird bent its head to his ear again, and I could see its beak moving. It *was* speaking to him.

"First years aren't allowed through the portal during their first semester," the prefect said flatly.

"But Lyssa needs to buy her books and robes, or she'll be in trouble."

"Bit late for that, isn't it? The semester starts tomorrow."

"I didn't know about the academy until today," I said. "Besides, you said we couldn't go through during our first semester, right? But it's not our first semester yet."

The prefect narrowed his eyes, but I thought I saw a flicker of amusement in them.

"Very well, Lyssa Eldridge. You may go through. Wouldn't want you to be in trouble."

"And Kelsey?" I pressed. "Otherwise how will I know where to go and what to buy?"

"Like to push your luck, don't you? Alright, you can both go through. But I'll be keeping a close eye on you, Lyssa."

The look he was giving me wasn't entirely unpleasant, so I gave him what I hoped was an innocent smile, and stepped through the portal.

If I lived to be a hundred, I would never get used to the sensation of lifting my foot up in one town, and putting it down in entirely another. One moment, we were in the calm, dimly-lit confines of the corridor beside the main hall, then next we were in a bustling street, with sunlight beaming down on us, and people jostling all around us. None of them so much as looked twice at us stepping out from the middle of a wall, which told me everything I needed to know: they were all druids, too. We were in a magical town.

"Fantail Market is the best place to get your magical supplies," Kelsey said. "You can get pretty much everything you could ever want right here."

I could believe it. The street we were in was lined both sides with shops, and in the gaps between them dozens of street traders were hawking their wares. The window to my left was hung with chalices and cauldrons, and to my right a bookstore carrying books with titles like 'First Year Alchemy: Changing Perceptions' and 'A Hundred and One Uses for Dragon Dung'. I was trying to think of a single use for dragon dung when something brushed my leg. I look down and saw a tiny green figure – no taller than my knee – wearing a tattered white shirt and bent over a walking stick. Fierce yellow eyes stared up at me and the creature's wide forehead furrowed into a scowl as it caught me staring.

"What's the matter wit' yer, girl, have y' never seen a Leprechaun before?"

It shook its head in disgust and hobbled away, while I stared in its wake. I lost sight of it behind a large fountain, the centre of which appeared to be an ice sculpture of a mermaid tail.

"Why doesn't the sculpture melt?" I wondered aloud.

"Huh?" Kelsey followed the direction of my gaze. "Oh, it's enchanted. Actually, it's what the marketplace is named after – you know, fantail – and as long as the sculpture is still standing, it means everything is safe and well here."

"Cool."

"Come on," she said, tugging lightly on my sleeve. "We'd best not stay too long, or we'll miss dinner." And if her eyes lingered just a little too long on the window we were passing, hung with all manner of cuts of meat, well I figured she must just have missed lunch. Who was I to criticise a girl for having a healthy appetite?

I hurried along next to her, barely getting chance to look at all the shops we passed.

"We should get your robes first," she said. "Flounders is bound to be running a sale this close to the start of the semester."

A sale sounded good, given that my stipend was likely to be extremely modest, and it was also likely to have to last a while. Kelsey was right, I saw as we reached Flounders. The window was hung with banners that danced and twirled where they hung, advertising up to fifty percent off. A portrait of a man in one of them beckoned to me, almost causing me to walk right into a cloaked figure hurrying in the opposite direction, carrying what looked to be a heavy pile of books. I stuttered an apology as he glared at me.

It was a relief when we stepped inside and found it almost deserted, save for one bored-looking sales assistant, who pointed us in the direction of the Fire element cloak without bothering to glance up from whatever was occupying his attention behind the counter. I wondered if it was the dragon dung book.

I tried on several of the ridiculous looking red cloaks before Kelsey nodded in satisfaction and declared the one that just barely touched the ground as I walked was perfect. Perfect wouldn't have been my word of choice – it weighed an absolute tonne and was insanely hot. I pulled it off with relief which was short-lived: Kelsey had already plucked half a dozen skirts and blouses from a rack and was shoving me towards the changing rooms. I tried them on with an air of resignation. The whole thing reminded me entirely too much of school shopping with my parents and my little sis– Wait, if mum and dad weren't my birth parents, did that mean Holly wasn't my sister?

"Hello, earth to Lyssa?"

I snapped back to my senses to see Kelsey waving a hand in front of my face.

"I'm sorry, what?"

"I said, we should pay for this stuff and get a move on."

We dumped my small mound of clothing in front of the bored clerk, who rang it up and declared the total was eight solarins, while the clothes folded themselves into a tidy pile. My mouth popped open as I watched. I *had* to learn how to do that.

"How do I, uh, pay?" I asked, not quite able to wrench my eyes away from the answer to all my laundry-related prayers.

"Hold your hand out," the clerk said, with a roll of his eyes. I stretched my hand out tentatively towards him. "Palm *down*."

I flipped my hand over, feeling my face turning pink. A blast of heat tingled against my palm but it wasn't entirely unpleasant. I looked more closely at the desk and saw a small crystal embedded into it: the source of the heat. It stopped as suddenly as it started, leaving me with my hand stretched over the desk and a clerk looking at me like I was the biggest idiot who'd ever crossed his threshold.

"You can take your hand back now."

"Oh. Right."

I thrust my hand back into my pocket and grabbed my bags from the counter, then made my way with

Kelsey back onto the street. I recognised the Dragondale uniform on the trio of girls walking past the store, and was about to call out a greeting when one of them turned and caught sight of us. Her pretty face crumpled into a sneer and she flicked her blonde hair over her shoulder.

"Oh, look," she said to one of her friends, "Dragondale has let in another charity case. Having to shop at Flounders, how pathetic. Next they'll be offering places to beggars."

The three of them erupted into laughter. I gritted my teeth and my hands curled into fists at my sides. I was *not* a charity case. Something touched my arm and I was about to shake it off irritably when I realised it was Kelsey's hand.

"Lyssa, leave it. She's not worth it."

"Yeah, leave it, charity case," the blonde said, her blue eyes flashing with amusement.

"What are you even doing here?" Kelsey said. "The prefect wasn't allowing first years through the portal."

"You obviously don't know who I am." The blonde looked her up and down. "When your father is as rich as mine is, you don't have to follow the same rules as the riffraff. No prizes for guessing how you two got through – you must have *begged* the prefect. Good practice for your future."

She laughed again and three trio flounced off with their hands full of expensive-looking bags and boxes. I didn't bother to keep the look of disgust off my face as I watched them go. Rich brats. Turned out you found them in all walks of life, and they were all as bad as each other.

"Forget about them. Come on, let's get the rest of your stuff."

Chapter Six

Getting the rest of my stuff was easy enough, but forgetting about the blonde, not so much. Her annoyingly beautiful face with its arrogant sneer was still burned behind my eyelids when I woke up the following morning. The good news was Kelsey had been right – I was sharing a room with her. The bad news was it turned out she talked almost as much in her sleep as she did when she was awake, and between her and the blonde girl's taunts, I was absolutely exhausted by the time light was streaming into our dorm.

"Hurry up, Lyssa – we don't want to be late for our first class."

"Yeah, yeah, I'm up," I grumbled. By the time I *was* actually up and dressed, and looking half-way human – the best I was going to achieve on three hours' sleep – Kelsey had sorted both her and my books for the day, and was practically bouncing on the balls of her feet by the door.

"Alright, what's first?"

She looked down at her schedule, although I was sure she had it memorised by now.

"Elemental Manipulation 101 first, and then breakfast. Then we've got Botany, and Gaelic. Then this afternoon–"

"Gaelic? You've got to be kidding me."

"Gaelic is one of the primary magical languages for druids. It's absolutely essential you learn the fundamentals if you want to be able to cast effective spells and incantations. And charms, and– Well, there really are no limits to its use. I started learning it when I was eight."

"Eight? You mean I'm ten years behind?"

"I'm sure you'll pick it up. I know it seems complicated, but it's actually really straightforward once you get the basics."

"Let's just hope I excel enough in these other classes to make up for it. Who knows, maybe I have a natural flair for–" I glanced over her shoulder at the schedule, "–potions."

I chucked a bottle of water in my bag, then we headed out through the common room and followed a handful of other students who apparently had the same class as us.

"Oh, great," I groaned as I stepped into the classroom, nodding to a trio of girls who were sitting in the middle of the front row. The blonde and her friends. Figured they'd be in the same class as us.

"Oh, look," the blonde said, a hint of ice beneath her saccharine tones. "It's charity case. Did you manage to beg for all your books?"

"Oh, look," I mimicked her tone. "It's the bimbo. Too bad all your money can't buy you any class."

I shot her a sarcastic smile and brushed past her, knocking her elbow. It might have been childish, but I can't deny that it was satisfying to see her face turn purple with anger. I made it four steps towards the back of the room when I heard her voice.

"I heard she was summoned to Professor Talendale's office yesterday. They say the Tilimeuse Tree couldn't tell what her primary element is. She probably doesn't even have enough magic for it to register. I bet she gets kicked out before the end of the week."

I started to turn round, but Kelsey stopped me with an angry whisper.

"Not in our first lesson. Are you trying to get expelled?"

I took a slow, deep breath and kept moving. The room was quite small and there were only six rows of seats – thirty seats in total. I sank into one of several empty chairs in the back row – but four rows separating us wasn't enough for my liking. Four miles wouldn't have done it. Kelsey took the seat on my right, and a moment later, a pile of books dropped onto the table on my left. A tall, dark-haired guy had taken the seat.

"You really don't want to make an enemy of Felicity," he said. "On the other hand, it's nice to see her taken down a couple of pegs. I'm Sam."

He stretched out his hand and I shook it, feeling a little awkward.

"Lyssa. This is Kelsey. And trust me, I can't wait to teach her a little humility."

He chuckled.

"Felicity, humility? There's not enough magic in this whole academy to do that."

"Settle down, settle down, everyone," a shrill voice announced from the front of the room. It belonged to a tall, slender woman with long blonde hair that flowed down past her shoulders and settled half-way down her back. She wore a pale blue dress with long sleeves, and a blue robe that looked much lighter than mine. She unclasped the robe and hung it on the back of the door while the excited murmurs faded to near-silence.

This was it. My first class was about to begin. I was going to learn magic. Real life magic. Butterflies started to flutter in my stomach, and my excitement turned to anxiety. What if Felicity was right – what if I didn't have much magic? Or any at all – what if that incident in the clearing was a fluke, and my whole invitation here a mistake? I chewed my lip, then reached down for my bottle of water. My throat was suddenly parched.

The lecturer turned back to us.

"My name is Professor Swann. In my classroom you will learn the fundamental skill of controlling your primary elements. Those of you who show great flair will one day have the opportunity to master a second element."

She sniffed, and the look on her face suggested she didn't think very many of us would reach that standard.

"But first things first, a little housekeeping. Everyone will move back one row. Those in the back row will move to the front, where I can keep an eye on you."

Her mistrustful face fell on the five of us who'd taken up the back row, and I wasn't quite clear whether she had an issue with us personally, or just with anyone who chose to sit at the back. I hoped the latter. The last thing I needed was one of the lecturers taking a disliking to me on my first day. I gathered up my books and my bottle of water, snatched my robe up from the back of my chair, and traipsed through the aisle to the front row with as much good grace as I could muster – which was to say, not much. I caught the smirk on Felicity's face on the way past, from her new seat in the second row, removing any doubts I might have had. She'd known Professor Swann was going to do this. Probably a higher year had told her, trying to win her favour. And now she was sitting right behind me. Great. One of her friends whispered in her ear, and the three of them broke out in cackles.

"Quiet, quiet!" Professor Swann snapped as everyone settled into their new seats, and silence fell again. It was a little too much like being in school for my liking – not the nice, anonymous university experience I'd had planned. On the other hand, I was about to learn magic, so on balance, I wasn't complaining.

She glanced around the room, and her eyes settled on the bottle of water sitting on my desk. For a moment I thought I was about to get a lecture – and not the good kind – but instead she simply looked at the bottle, her face serene. The sealed lid burst off and I jumped back, almost toppling my chair, to the delight of Felicity and her cronies. I ignored her, staring at my bottle. A steady stream of water rose out of it like a ribbon, until there wasn't even a single drop left clinging to the plastic sides – it was all floating through the air in a single elegant strand. It twirled around the professor's head, and then gathered itself into a ball in front of her.

I watched, rapt, as the water twisted within the ball, like tiny waves hitting invisible rocks. She flicked her eyes to one side and the ball flung itself across the room, spinning and twisting as it raced through the air, stopping just inches short of a student's head. The boy gasped and flinched back, but the water was moving again, this time in a more leisurely fashion. The ball drifted towards me, and I fought the urge to reach out and touch it, succeeding only because my limbs were beyond my control right now, with so much wonder was I staring.

The water stopped above my bottle and then poured itself carefully back inside as though through a thin funnel, not spilling a drop. When it finally settled back into place, I stared at the bottle in amazement. It was just as full as it had been to start with.

"Those of you who make the effort will be rewarded with excellence," Professor Swann said, turning her eyes on us again. "Those who do not will find themselves failing this year. Elemental control is the foundation for all your magic. Fail to give it the respect it deserves, and all of your magic will be mediocre, at best."

"Those of us who have magic," I heard Felicity whisper behind me.

"Did you see the look on Liam's face?" one of her friends whispered back.

"I heard his father's taken a job as a janitor for the circle," the other one said, and I could hear the sneer in her voice. I tried to tune them out. I wasn't about to let them ruin my first class at Dragondale.

"Of course," the professor continued, her voice cutting across the whispers behind my back, "it takes many years of study to achieve control like that which you have just witnessed. Today, we will be starting with something more basic."

Well, that was a relief, and judging by the look on Sam's face beside me, I wasn't the only one who thought so. The professor held up her hand, palm facing us, and the centre of it glowed. I blinked, thinking it was a trick of the light, but as I watched the glow grew stronger, until it was a bright blue light that could have lit up half the room, if the fireballs in the corner weren't already doing that.

"Your magic comes from within. You must simply focus on your hand and *feel* your magic inside it."

Feel my magic? I shot Kelsey a bewildered look. How was I supposed to do that when I had no idea what magic even felt like?

"Excellent work, Felicity," Professor Swann said.

I glanced back over my shoulder to see Felicity's palm glowing with a soft yellow. That did it. If she could do it, I could do it. I stared down at my palm, willing it to glow red. It stayed resolutely skin-coloured.

"Told you she had no magic," a voice whispered from behind me, obviously meant for me to overhear.

"Like this." Kelsey showed me her palm, which had a dull red pulsing on its skin. I tried again, furrowing my brow with concentration.

"Everyone show me your palms. I will be coming round and instructing each of you."

Professor Swann started with the front row, of course. She worked her way along, giving advice to each student, whose hands invariably glowed brighter by the time she moved on. Of course, they'd all had glows to start with. When she reached mine, there still wasn't so much as a flicker.

"Focus, Ms Eldridge. You will achieve nothing in my class if you do not apply yourself."

My face flushed red under the undeserved criticism, but my palm did not.

"You must reach inside yourself and focus on the fire within."

I thought back to when my rejection letter caught fire in the clearing. I'd been annoyed, disappointed in myself, and bitter that they'd turned me down. Even a little angry when Toby had scratched me, unprovoked. I summoned all those feelings to mind, and willed them into my hand.

"Keep trying, I have no doubt that you will get it. Eventually." The last word spoken with a sigh that made me question her not doubting me. "I will return to you after assisting the other students."

She moved on to Sam, whose palm was giving a slight red glow. He must be a Fire, too. And better than me. Shocker. Apparently, I was the only one who couldn't master the simplest exercise imaginable. Even Liam had a faint red glow pulsing on his palm.

"Very good, Felicity," I heard the professor say as she moved along the row behind me. "Why don't you practice increasing and decreasing the strength of your glow? We were going to work on that in our next lesson, but I see no point in holding you back."

I've always been a glutton for punishment, so I turned round in time to see the smug look on Felicity's face. Of course she excelled in class. I was going to have to stop calling her a bimbo. How annoying.

"Paisley, that's very good," the professor said, inspecting Felicity's dark-haired friend's palm. "You could be a little more consistent around the edges. See how it's just a little fainter here?"

She pointed to a spot on Paisley's palm, and I turned away before I ran the risk of puking. Everyone was better than I was. Maybe Felicity was right. Maybe I didn't belong here. I should have just carried on studying to resit my normal exams, in my normal, non-magical world, which was clearly where I belonged.

"You'll get it," Kelsey whispered as soon as Swann was out of earshot.

"What if I don't?" I whispered back. She gave me a sympathetic smile.

"Don't worry about them," Sam said, not taking as much care to keep his voice quiet – he clearly wasn't so terrified of getting in trouble with Swann as Kelsey was. "Some people round here have been practicing for years, even if they're not supposed to have been."

He gave Felicity a meaningful look. She stared daggers back at him, then turned her eyes on me.

"I hope you got a good returns policy on those books. You're not going to be needing them much longer."

I was definitely going to punch her this time. My hands bunched into fists, because dammit, I'd dealt with people like her my entire life, and I wasn't about to back down to some rich bitch who thought her daddy's money made her better than everyone else.

"Lyssa!" I heard Kelsey's gasp beside me. I thought she just didn't want me getting into trouble by rearranging Felicity's too-pretty face, but when she grabbed my fist and flipped it over, I saw what had her so worked up. There was a red glow seeping through my clenched fingers. I opened my hand and stared at the bright red circle sitting in the centre of my palm. My mouth popped open in surprise and delight, and the flare disappeared as quickly as it had come. I glanced around, but apparently no-one other than me, Kelsey and Sam had seen it.

Dammit. I was never going to convince Swann I'd pulled it off. I slumped in my seat and went back to staring at my palm, willing it to turn red again.

Chapter Seven

I didn't manage to make my palm glow again for the rest of the lesson, but I knew it had happened, and unlike the letter catching fire in the clearing, other people had seen it, too – so I knew I wasn't imagining it. The Tilimeuse Tree was right. I was a druid, and I belonged at the Dragondale Academy of Druidic Magic.

We all chattered excitedly on the way to breakfast – taken in the main hall, with each elemental house seated together in one quarter. The stage Professor Talendale had addressed us from yesterday now held a counter with a line of students queuing up, each holding a plate. Me, Kelsey, and Sam each snagged a plate from the pile and joined the end of the line. There were about thirty students in front of us, and only one person serving at the counter. I had a feeling we were going to be in for a long wait, but the queue moved surprisingly quickly.

"So, you never even knew magic existed before you came here?" Sam said, staring at me in bemusement as we neared the counter. I shook my head.

"Nope. I thought the whole thing was a joke when I got my acceptance letter."

"Well, I think you're doing great." He cast a look in the direction of the Air quarter. "So don't let Felicity get to you. She'll get bored soon enough and pick on someone else. There's a reason they call them airheads."

"He's right, you know," Kelsey piped up, as she neared the front of the queue and set her plate on the counter. "Not many people could summon their element within a day of learning about it. Felicity has had her whole life to practice that sort of thing. Not that we're supposed to... but everyone does, just a little. And some people do more than a little because they think the rules don't apply to them. Just wait until we start learning new things. I bet she won't find it half so easy then."

"Well, if it isn't the two outcasts."

I turned round and found myself face to face with Felicity.

"Although I'm surprised to see *you* wasting your time with these two losers, Sam. I thought you had better breeding than that."

"You thought?" Sam said. "That must have been a novel experience for an airhead."

She glowered at him, and for a moment I thought she was actually going to stamp her foot like a spoiled princess. Instead, she plastered a nasty smile on her face and elbowed past me.

"Don't mind if I go first, do you, charity case?"

"Be my guest." I smiled sweetly. "It might help you learn the difference between breeding and class."

Her smile tightened as she slapped her plate down on the counter.

"Bagels," she said without so much as a glance at the man behind the counter. "And a melon slice."

The man muttered a few words and the food appeared on her plate. Just appeared, out of thin air. I waited for her to pick up her plate and saunter away before I whispered to Kelsey.

"Did he just create that?"

"Not exactly," she replied, not bothered to whisper. "All the food comes from the kitchen, but it's more like a storeroom. If the raw ingredients are there, he can transform them into whatever you want. Like if you wanted steak, he could cast the spell and it would appear, fully cooked." She broke off and gave him a smile. "Kitchen mages are incredibly skilled. But, if there was no beef in the kitchen, he couldn't simply conjure it from nowhere."

"Wow."

The kitchen mage was giving me an amused look as Kelsey explained everything to me, apparently in no rush – probably because we were the last students in the queue.

"You must be the newgen," he said. I shook my head.

"Nope. It's a long story."

"Well, I'm here breakfast, lunch and dinner, five days a week. A word to the wise though: the weekend kitchen mage is new, and she's not all that good, so don't order anything to complicated from her. Now, what can I get you?"

Sam got some cereal and I opted for just a slice of toast, because my stomach was churning too much to even think of eating more. Meanwhile, Kelsey ordered a full English – sausage, eggs, bacon, toast, tomatoes – and it smelled as good as anything I'd ever seen on a plate. I looked Kelsey's lean body up and down, wondering where she was planning to put it all, but by the end of breakfast she returned an empty plate to the counter, which is more than could be said for my feeble efforts. I felt a little guilty when I returned my virtually untouched toast to the kitchen mage, but he just gave me an understanding smile and told me I'd settle in soon enough. I hoped he was right, because a two second red glow in my palm hardly amounted to earth-shattering magic, and I was already feeling sick at the thought of my next elemental manipulation class – which apparently were a daily staple here at Dragondale.

Gaelic was every bit as terrible as I'd feared. Everyone was miles ahead of me, and Professor Thorne went so far as to suggest I might want to have extra lessons with him at the weekends – as if my workload wasn't heavy enough. The only good thing was that the year group was divided differently for that lesson, so I didn't have to put up with Felicity. For that reason alone, I could almost get to like it. But not quite.

I was so wrapped up in my lessons, and how terrible I was at most of them, that it wasn't until after dinner that I remembered I had other problems to worry about. The three of us were sitting in the Fire common room – Kelsey studying from our Botany textbook, and Sam staring up at the ceiling, declaring his brain had melted somewhere in Druidic Law – when I wondered what druids actually did to make money. I had a feeling the academy stipend wasn't going to last me long, and besides, I didn't want to be relying on their generosity for the rest of the year.

"So, how do I go about getting a job?" I asked.

"If this is because of everything Felicity was spouting earlier," Sam started, but I cut him off with a shake of my head.

"It's not. Besides, it'll be a good way for me to learn about our world, right?"

"A better way would be hanging out with us and not working," Sam pointed out. "I mean, we're basically experts on all things magic."

I pulled out a cushion I'd been leaning on and tossed it at him.

"I saw your attempts in Potions today. You're not an expert on anything."

"Ouch, burn."

"About the only thing I can burn," I grumbled.

"You'll get it," Kelsey said, setting her textbook aside. "Just give it time. And I heard Professor Alden was looking for a couple of first years to help out with the academy's livestock. We've got class with her tomorrow."

"What sort of livestock?" I asked, because truth be told, I had a hard time imagining the Dragondale academy kept chickens and rabbits. Kelsey just smiled.

"Trust me, it'll be a great way to learn more about our world."

*

If there's one thing I've learned, it's that you should never trust anyone who says 'trust me'. Life at the academy proved to be no exception. When we traipsed down to the barn while the sun was still rising the following morning, cloaks wrapped around us for warmth, wearing the thickest gloves we owned and still shivering, Kelsey and Sam were suspiciously quiet.

We were in a mixed class again, meaning I once more had the dubious pleasure of Felicity's company. She was smiling nastily as we arrived in the clearing outside a large barn, painted red and gold and looking pristine.

The professor emerged from inside it before either of us could get any decent insults in, and clapped her gloved hands. She was a short woman with a round face and red cheeks, and her hair, a mottled mix of brown and grey, was tied back.

"Good morning, everyone. I'm Professor Alden. Once a week you will join me to be instructed in the art and science of paranormal creatures – that is to say, creatures not recognised by the average mundane. Some of you may think this class is less important than the likes of elemental manipulation and spellcraft, but I assure you your grade in my class carries every bit as much weight as the rest of your studies. Fail here, and you will not progress to your next year."

At her warning, a few of the guys at the back stopped messing around and started to pay attention. I chewed my lip, because I was still pretty convinced that when Professor Alden pulled those doors open, we wouldn't be looking at a barn load of cute bunnies.

"Some of you may be aware that Dragondale Academy has a reputation as one of the finest producers of hippogryffs in the entire magical community, and I can assure you that reputation is not undeserved."

I raised a hand, since no-one else seemed about to ask the question. The professor nodded to me.

"Yes, Miss…?"

"Eldridge. Lyssa Eldridge," I said. "Um, what's a hippogryff?"

There was a burst of laughter from behind me, coming from somewhere in Felicity's direction, and a few others joined in. My face turned red.

"Yes, yes, very funny. Oh, you're serious." Alden's eyes widened in surprise, as though I'd said I had no idea what a cow was. "Well, the hippogryff is a druid-created hybrid between a gryphon and a horse, most notably used in Itealta."

She gave me another nod as though that cleared everything up instead of raising at least another half-dozen questions, but I figured I might as well just wait and see for myself.

"Follow me, everyone."

We turned and trudged towards the barn in her wake – most of the group because they were half-awake, me because I was still trying to decipher Alden's answer.

"A gryphon is a kind of mix between an eagle and a lion," Sam said as we walked. "It's got a beak and wings, and talons at its front end, and the back end of a lion. A lion is—"

"I know what a lion is," I snapped, a little more irritably than I'd intended. A look of hurt flashed across Sam's face and I felt like the biggest jerk on campus. Way to treat the people who are actually on your side, Lyssa. "Sorry."

"It's fine. It's a lot to take in, right? Anyway, Itealta is a sport, like… well, I'm not really sure what the mundane equivalent is."

He looked at Kelsey who just shrugged.

"Each house has a team. We'll show you."

Professor Alden paused with her hand on the barn door and fixed us with a stern glare.

"There will be absolutely no hijinks or horseplay inside this barn. The gryffs are extremely sensitive to strangers, and though these ones are tame, they will still deliver a nasty bite or kick if startled or provoked. Anyone losing a finger will have marks deducted for this class. Am I clear?"

I didn't think I was the only one who gulped, but I was too busy staring at the barn to be sure. No-one told me coming to the academy was going to be dangerous.

"The gryffs have been stabled overnight due to the weather, so they will likely be a little irritable this morning. Each of you collect a food bucket on your way through, but absolutely no opening stable doors or attempting to handle the gryffs until you are told otherwise."

Alden swung the doors open, and I peered past her into the dimly lit barn. The musty odour of animals and straw wafted out, and then my nose wrinkled as it caught a sharp, acrid scent. I looked down at the row of twenty stainless steel buckets. As we got closer, I peered inside one and saw it was filled with whole fish – herrings and mackerel and sardines, heads, tails, guts and all. I recoiled from the sight, muttering under my breath.

"Guess they're not heavy on the horse side."

"Gryffs are carnivorous," Kelsey told me, picking up a bucket and handing it to me, then getting another for herself. "They prefer birds and small mammals, but they also have a taste for fish."

"Careful one doesn't eat you," Felicity sneered as she elbowed past me to get her bucket. "But then, I've heard they prefer a rich diet, so you're probably safe."

I glared at her back as she strutted off along the aisle, with Paisley and Cecelia trailing in her wake like obedient puppies. Or laughing hyenas.

My anger was quickly forgotten when all along the rows on either side of the aisle, beaked faces appeared over the stable doors. A small gasp escaped my lips and I edged closer to the nearest one. Large, intelligent eyes followed my movements, set in a feathered, bird-like face, with ears that flickered at the sound of my approach. This one's feathers were black, each quill edged in a fine gold outline. It quirked its head to one side and chattered its beak a little as it looked at the bucket in my hand.

"Wow," I breathed. "It's beautiful."

The creature let out a quiet mewl, and preened, as though it could sense my appreciation. It stretched out its neck, lowering its oddly elegant beaked face towards me. I set my bucket on the floor and stretched a trembling hand through the air towards it, until my fingers were mere inches from brushing its porcelain smooth beak.

Further up the aisle came a loud clatter. I started and jumped back, twisting my head round to see a toppled bucket with its contents spread across the floor. The gryff let out a screech that seemed to burn my eardrums. I clamped my hands over my ears with a gasp and it screeched again, snapping at the air with its hooked beak. Massive wings rose at its slides and flapped in agitation and I heard a hoof kick the side of the stall. Its eyes were wide, showing their whites and it flapped its wings again, this time rearing up on its hind legs and showing me a flash of scaled talons where front hooves should have been. I forced my hands from my ears and held them low and open.

"Easy. Easy, boy," I said, stretching my words out and keeping my voice as calm as I could. I had no idea with no idea whether it was male or female, but I hoped it wasn't smart enough to know the difference. "You're okay. Steady, steady."

The flapping stopped but it eyed me distrustfully, still flashing its whites, and pranced on the spot.

"I know. I know. It's okay. Here, want a fish?"

I crouched down without breaking our eye contact and reached into the bucket. My hand closed around something cold and slimy, and I drew the fish out. The creature's eyes immediately twitched to the food and then back to mine.

"Yeah, that's better," I soothed. "Here you go."

I stood and held the fish out and the gryff shook out its wings one last time, settling them back into position on its shoulders, and reached out, snapping the fish from my hand. It tilted its head back and swallowed in one gulp, then stretched its head out and butted my hand.

"Alright, alright," I said with a chuckle. "I'll get more."

It wasn't until I stooped to grab the bucket that I realised the barn had gone utterly silent – no traipse of footsteps, no laughter or chatter from the students, no Alden barking instructions. Every single pair of eyes was on me.

"Absolutely incredible," Alden said as she broke away from the group of staring students. "Never have I seen anyone calm an agitated hippogryff so quickly. And you still have all your fingers, I presume?"

I glanced down at my intact hands and a smile crept onto my face.

"Very good, Miss Eldridge. Do not keep your gryff waiting. That goes for the rest of you, too. Quickly now, back to work."

I hefted up the rest of the bucket and smiled at the stunning creature. And if I wasn't very much mistaken, the gryff smiled back.

Once the gryffs were fed, Professor Alden showed us how to put on a head collar and lead the creatures from their stalls and out into the expansive of fields that surrounded the academy. Two boys were kicked, and a girl was bitten, but other than that we managed it without incident. My gryff followed by my side, tugging gently at strands of hair on my head as we walked. The professor just watched on in quiet amazement, which I took to mean the gryff wasn't about to take a chunk out of my skull.

One by one, Alden took the creatures and released them into the fields, some galloping, others flying, until only mine was left, prancing impatiently by my side, and occasionally shaking out its massive wings.

"Very well, Lyssa," said Professor Alden. "When you're ready, take Stormclaw's headcollar off, the exact same way I did, and let him go."

"You... you want me to do it?" I eyed the gryff's hooked beak warily. Several of the other beasts had taken snaps at Alden when she unclipped their headcollars – and she knew exactly how to handle them. I didn't particularly rate my chances of managing it unscathed.

"Yes, go on. You seem to have a way with him."

I sucked in a deep breath and blew it out slowly, then stretched up a hand towards the creature's face.

"Alright, then. Nice and steady," I said softly, as much to myself as the gryff. "No need for anyone to get bitten."

As if understanding my intentions, Stormclaw lowered his head towards me, so that I didn't have to go up on tiptoes to reach him. My fingers brushed against his feathers, smooth and silky to the touch. For a moment I forgot all about his vicious hooked beak, and reputation for cropping first-year fingers, and ran my fingers along his crest, caressing him. He leaned into my touch, emitting a low, thrumming sound in his throat that almost reminded me of a cat purring.

I unclipped the headcollar and slipped it off, keeping it well clear of his legs... or, er, talons. I didn't want him to get tangled up or hurt, not after he'd so considerately resisted the urge to trim my fingers. Instead of running right off to join the rest of his herd, he lowered his head and butted me in the chest. I staggered back a step, off balance, and he cocked his head to one side, blinking as he watched me. He butted me again, more gently this time, and I couldn't help but chuckle. He might look fearsome, but he was behaving like an overgrown puppy. I scratched his long, feathered ears and he made the thrumming sound again.

"Go on," I told him, looking off to the rest of the herd. "Get out of here."

He gave a single squawk, then cantered off towards the group. After a dozen strides, he flapped his black and gold wings, and took to the skies, screeching loudly.

"Well, I have never…" said the professor. "I do believe he has chosen you."

Chapter Eight

It was a relief to know that I wasn't completely useless at everything I turned my hand to inside the academy walls, or, well, outside them in this case. Felicity had made a snide comment about it being a servant's work, but not even she could completely smother the look of surprise at how well Stormclaw had responded to me.

"Of course," I overheard her saying on our way to breakfast, "I have half a dozen hippogryffs at home. I bet charity case couldn't even afford a feather."

Her little cluster of hangers-on dissolved into sniggers at that, but I didn't care. Professor Alden had said I was a natural and told me I could help out with them to earn some money. She'd even said something about learning to ride – not that I was sure that was such a great idea. I mean, they might not all be quite so keen on me as Stormclaw had been. Sure, the academy hospital wing could regrow fingers in a matter of hours, but somehow I didn't think that would make losing them any less painful, nor was I in any hurry to find out.

Kelsey and Sam had said gryffs tended be cantankerous creatures, and it was rare they'd allow strangers to handle them – much less stroke them the way Stormclaw had allowed me. The rest of the day's lessons passed in a bit of a blur. I was terrible in elemental manipulation again, and I didn't have a clue what was going on for most of Gaelic class, but eventually the end of the day came around. We had two hours before dinner, and while the others headed to the common room to make a start on the heaps of assignments we'd already been given, I grabbed a bottle of water and tugged on my cloak, then headed down to the barn.

Alden was already waiting for me when I got there, and she beamed when she saw me.

"Ah, Lyssa, excellent. I'm thrilled you decided to take me up on my offer."

I eyed her warily. No-one had been that happy to see me since I arrived at the academy.

"Now, we keep a lot of different species here at Dragondale, but I intend to keep you working with my herd of gryffs." She headed inside the barn and I walked alongside her, breathing in the heady scent of gryffs again. "If you show as much natural talent as you did this morning, and you work hard, then I'm sure I can keep you busy for the rest of the semester. The year, if you want."

The closest stalls, twelve in all, were occupied with a dozen gryffs of all colours – one solid black, another solid white, and a couple white with brown patches on their hides and faces. A pair of them were deep shades of

83

brown, and another still was black with a multi-coloured sheen to his feathers wherever they caught the light, like a magpie. None bore black feathers lined in gold.

"Where's Stormclaw?" I asked, peering into the stalls further back in case he was lurking there.

"Out in the fields still. These are the Earth Itealta team gryffs. They have a practice scheduled for this evening."

"Which team is Stormclaw on?"

Alden shook her head.

"He's not. He put his last three riders in the hospital. He's too dangerous to ride. Shame. He's a beautiful specimen and as agile as any gryff I've seen, but he just won't accept a rider. Now, enough talk. The team will be arriving soon, and we need to get their mounts prepared."

That basically involved fitting each gryff with a saddle – much the same as the sort you'd put on a horse, but with a massive saddle horn at the front – and attaching a pair of reins to their specially-adapted head collars. Gryffs weren't ridden with a bit in their mouths, Alden explained, due to the shape of their beaks: the rider had to rely on their animal's training and willingness to please the rider. Having seen their tempers this morning, I was amazed that anyone ever managed to control one. They seemed pretty wilful.

Despite that, we had all twelve tacked up and ready for their riders by the time the team joined us. They took their time greeting the creatures, and to my amazement not one of them took a snap at their riders as they mounted.

The game of Itealta was possibly the most bizarre thing I'd witnessed so far, and that was saying something. The team was made up of eight riders, plus three substitutes and a reserve, and the goal was to score goals by tossing a soccer-sized leather ball, with metal handles on each side, through a vertical hoop atop a pole thirty foot in the air. The riders had to carry the ball, or pass it between their teammates, while the other team attempted to snatch it from them – either by intercepting a pass, or by trying to rip the ball out of their opponent's arms.

As I watched, one student attempted the latter 'steal', almost succeeding in unseating both riders – which in itself would be worrying enough, but given that the whole thing was happening twenty foot in the air, with their gryffs flying shoulder to shoulder... I winced and tried to look away, but my eyes refused to leave the spectacle, certain that one of them would tumble to the ground and be carted off to the medical wing. I was wrong. The stealing rider gripped the ball with one hand, and with the other, squeezed his reins whilst pressing his legs to his steed, and the gryff wheeled away, attempting to use the force of the massive flying beast to rip the ball from his opponent's hands. The other rider was forced to choose between relinquishing possession of the ball, and being ripped clean from his saddle, to fall to the solid ground beneath. For a moment I thought he was going to cling to the ball regardless, but at the last second it was torn free from his fingers, leaving him half in, half out of his saddle while the attacking rider wheeled away, towards the hoop at the far end of the field. The defending rider's mouth moved in what I was pretty sure was a cuss word that was snatched away by the wind, and spun his mount round to give chase, the speed of the turn throwing him back into his seat.

If I had to choose a word to describe the sport, I'd be torn between 'exhilarating' and 'absolutely certifiable'. Well, okay, that was two words… and yet it was still the one I'd go with. Somehow, and I don't know how, an hour later the session ended without anyone having needed to pay a trip to the hospital wing – though there'd probably be a few bruises in the morning. Seriously, if this was the druidic world's idea of sport, then I was definitely signing up to be a cheerleader, not a jock.

When their practice ended, the team headed off, with their captain critiquing their individual performances the whole time. I watched them go with a shake of my head, then Professor Alden showed me how to untack the gryffs. By the time all twelve were done, I was getting the hang of snatching my hands back in time to avoid being bitten. The professor cast an eye over the untacked gryffs tethered to the fence and nodded her approval.

"Excellent. Let's get them out to the field to join the rest of the herd, and then you'll be about done."

It was not as simple as she made it sound. The gryffs were feeling excitable after their training session, and they all danced around on the end of their lead ropes, kicking up their legs and shaking out their wings. A couple took snaps at each other, so that we had to make sure there was a good distance between them at all times – which meant we had to make half a dozen trips down to the paddocks and back. By the time that was done, I felt like I'd run a marathon, and my entire body was aching.

"Good work," the professor said as we lugged the last of the saddles back into the barn. "Yes, that one on the very end rack. Yes, that's the one."

I hefted the saddle onto the rack with a grunt, and glanced at my watch with a stifled yawn. What I really wanted was to sleep, but if I got a move on, I'd just about make it to the main hall before the kitchen mage packed up for the evening. There was nothing like grappling with twelve cantankerous gryffs to work up an appetite.

"Just a moment, Lyssa," Professor Alden said, wiping her hands clean on her robes in a way that I was sure would have horrified Professor Swann. "One last thing before you finish for the evening. Grab that bucket, please."

I swallowed my groan of protest by fantasising over what I was going to spend my first lot of wages on – and if I was going to be honest, school books were *not* top of the list – and picked up the bucket, casting a cursory glance at its contents.

That was a mistake.

I gagged, almost dropping it right back on the floor. The only instinct that made me keep a grip on the handle was the one that said I definitely did not want to risk its contents spilling over my shoes.

"What is that?" I wheezed in between gagging and retching.

"What does it look like?" the professor asked mildly, pulling on a pair of thick gloves covered in some sort of greenish-blue scales.

I decided not to chance another look in the bucket, and just went off my initial impression.

"Guts and organs, and… something that smells vile."

"Very good. That'll be the lung you're smelling. You'll get used to it. There's some meat in there, too."

I absolutely did not want to get used to the smell of anything inside the metal bucket, nor did I particularly want to know what sort of 'meat' it was. In fact, I'd started to suspect it was a whole can of worms I should never have opened. Still though, as I hurried after Alden, trying to keep my nose away from the sloshing red mix, I couldn't help myself from asking,

"But Professor... What eats this?"

I shouldn't have asked. I knew I shouldn't have asked the moment the words slipped out of my mouth, and the twinkle in the professor's eye just confirmed what I knew.

"We don't normally let the first years meet him. Or the second years. Or most of the third years, really... but, well, he really is a magnificent beast. This way."

She pressed her hand and pulsed an energy password into the door of what looked like an old shed, but it might as well have been the wardrobe to Narnia. I stepped through and found myself in a small stone building, one side of which was constructed entirely of heavy metal bars. Beyond them was a jungle that had not been outside the shed.

"Ares!" the professor called. "Dinner time!"

She took the bucket from me as I stared out in wonder. How many more buildings were there like this one? How big was the academy, truly? But my mind was soon ripped from the topic as a flying, tan-coloured beast swooped from the sky, landing with a thud that made the ground shake beneath my feet. At a distance, I'd thought he was a hippogryff, but up close I could see how wrong

I was. This creature was far more heavily set, his entire body armoured in thick slabs of muscle. His front end was bird-like, just like the hippogryffs, but that was where the resemblance ended. His back feet were paws, not hooves, and each was bigger that my head, and tipped with sharp, curved claws that were longer than my fingers. His tail was a thick rope, like a leopard… or a lion.

"Ares is a gryphon," Professor Alden announced proudly, confirming my suspicion. "Half eagle, half lion. One of only a handful left in the country, probably the world. He sired half of our herd of gryffs."

Well, at least that explained why they were so cantankerous.

"Is he… Is he safe?" I asked, taking a tentative step towards the massive beast, who was regarding me with his head tilted to one side.

"Oh, no, dear – he'd eat you as soon as look at you. Wouldn't you, sweetheart?"

I took a hasty step back, while the professor eyed him with almost maternal pride. He screeched at her with what might have been affection – if I was to give him the benefit of the doubt – and she thrust the bucket through the bars. He shoved his head into the bucket, tearing it from Alden's grip, then came up again with a mouthful of something I didn't care to identify. He tipped his head back and swallowed it in a single gulp, then screeched at us again, flapping his wings in a show of aggression before snatching up another mouthful.

"Isn't he something?" the professor said, nearly breathless with admiration.

He was something, alright. Deadly. Crazy. Terrifying. Take your pick. One thing was for sure – Itealta didn't seem nearly so dangerous as it had half an hour ago.

Chapter Nine

Today we will be focussing on illusion magic – specifically, glamours."

Professor Atherton stood at the front of the class and peered out at us. A couple of groans met his words, although for my part I was just confused. I'd been at the academy a couple of weeks now, but I still had no idea what half of the things the professors talked about actually were. Our spellcraft class was no exception.

"Now, for those of you who do not know, a glamour is a spell that disguises your appearance. A trained magic user will be able to see through your glamour – and I'm not just talking about druids – so the primary use for this spell is outside of the magical community. With sufficient training, you will be able to transform your entire appearance. Today, however, we shall start small. You will cast a glamour on your hair to change its colour."

As Atherton spoke, his jet black hair turned white, then light brown, then red and finally back to black again, all without him so much as pausing in his speech.

"That's so cool," I whispered to Kelsey.

"Glamour is just the best skill," she whispered back.

"You're such a pair of girls," Sam said with a groan. "Who cares about changing your hair colour?"

"Ah, Mr Devlin. Since I know you wouldn't be talking during my lecture, I can only presume you were volunteering to go first. Stand up, please."

Sam groaned again as the rest of the class laughed, then got to his feet with a lopsided grin and a slight flush to his cheeks beneath his blond hair.

"The glamour relies purely on visualisation and intention. Remember, you are not changing the colour of your hair, you are merely projecting an illusion. The most common technique is to imagine the illusion you wish to project on top of your own image, and then imbue that image with your magic. You may begin, Mr Devlin."

Sam squeezed his eyes shut and his forehead furrowed with the intensity of his concentration. After a moment, he opened his eyes and looked around at us.

"Well?"

"Not completely terrible, Mr Devlin," Atherton conceded. And, looking closer, I could see that Sam's short blond hair was indeed a couple of shades darker. It wasn't as dramatic as what the professor had done to his own hair, but it was still bound to be better than anything I could manage.

"Sit down. Perhaps next time you'd like to attempt something a little more challenging – as Ms Hutton has done."

I threw a look in Felicity's direction and sure enough, there she was, preening under her long locks, which were now a coloured flaming red that made Kelsey's look dull.

"Very good, Ms Hutton. Five points for air."

"I was trying for black," said Sam from the corner of his mouth. I chuckled under my breath.

"Is something amusing you, Ms Eldridge?"

Uh-oh. This was only my second class with Atherton so far, but he'd taken a disliking to me. Actually, he seemed to dislike anyone outside of his own elemental house – air – but in my case it was particularly severe.

"No, Profes–" I started, but he slammed his hand down on his desk.

"I will not have your insolence in my class. If you cannot apply yourself, then you will leave. Immediately."

"But I–"

"Out! Now."

Unbelievable. I gaped at him for a long moment before pushing myself to my feet. I stuffed my books and water into my bag under the glaring eyes of Atherton and swung it onto my shoulder, then stalked from the room. It was times like this I despised the enchanted doors – I really wanted to slam it shut behind me. Instead, as it swung serenely closed, I heard Felicity's icy laughter. The noise grated on my nerves like nails down a chalkboard. Gritting my teeth, I stomped down the hallway... then I realised I was acting like a child and stopped, taking a moment to draw in a long, steady breath, then blow it back out again. Atherton wanted to play favourites. So what? Sure, glamour was a really cool trick that I wanted to learn, but who cared? It wasn't like his class was the only way I could learn it. And it wasn't like I didn't have better things to do than learn dumb tricks, anyway. In fact, Alden had given me the name of a book about the care of hippogryffs I could check out of the library, but I hadn't had a chance to get there yet. Might as well head straight there since I had an hour until everyone else finished for lunch.

I hurried along the deserted corridors, trying to recall the way to the library, which was much harder without Kelsey to help me. It wasn't exactly a favourite hangout of mine. I didn't think books were going to be much use when it came to my nebulous control of my newfound powers. And whilst the history of magic was a whole lot more interesting than the industrial revolution, it still didn't feature high up on the list of things I spent my time doing.

I'd walked the length of six completely unfamiliar corridors before I was forced to admit it. I was lost. Totally, irredeemably, hopelessly lost. I'd never seen this part of the academy before, and judging by the cobwebs hanging in every corner, it wasn't well frequented. The fireballs hanging near the ceiling were dim, like the magic holding them there had been long neglected. It was so quiet down here that I could hear the rustle of my clothing as I moved. And there was a really odd smell – not a pleasant one. Kind of like something had crawled down here and died. About ten years ago.

The further I went, the worse the smell got, until I could practically taste the cloying odour in the back of my throat. I took another step, and gagged, covering my mouth. That did it. There was absolutely no way the library was anywhere near here. I was turning back.

Something brushed against my leg.

I screamed and leapt so far sideways that I collided with the dusty stone wall, immediately tangling myself in cobwebs. I pushed away and spun round, backing away from…

Toby. It was Toby. The wampus. A nervous laugh slipped from lips as my pounding heart started to steady itself. At least he was in his cat form – if I'd stumbled across the massive, heavily muscled creature with six legs and two tails, I reckon I'd have about had a heart attack.

"What are you doing down here?" I asked him, then immediately regretted opening my mouth as I breathed in another lungful of the toxic odour. There was, of course, no reply, just the echo of my words bouncing off the walls.

"We should get out of here."

The wampus meowed and then started trotting off in front of me, back the way I'd come. I shrugged. I'd done crazier things than follow a shapeshifting cat along a deserted corridor recently.

His four legs were faster than my two, and each time we rounded a corner I fell further behind him. Soon I was jogging to keep up, and a half-dozen turns later I lost sight of him completely. I skidded to a stop, listening for any sound of the supernatural beast. Nothing. Except for… I cocked my head. Yes. There were voices. That way.

I headed towards them, relief making me giddy.

"What are you doing here, Charity?" a voice sneered. Felicity. Great. I guess that relief had been a little premature. "And what on earth happened to your robes? Have you been rolling around in the gutter again?"

Paisley and Cecelia burst into laughter like it was the best joke they'd heard all semester. They had low standards. I fixed her with my most cutting stare.

"As opposed to rolling around with every guy who looks at you twice?"

Felicity's cheeks turned red and she narrowed her eyes at me.

"What are you doing skulking around outside the Air common room, anyway?" she demanded. "I'm going to report you to Professor Atherton."

"For what? Walking down a corridor?"

"You've obviously been up to no good. Although apparently that's all you're capable of." She sniffed. "Come on, girls, there's a funny smell around here."

She gave me a pointed look and then flounced past me, taking care not to get too close – presumably in case being working class was contagious. Paisley and Cecelia gave me looks that were almost as dirty as my clothes, and hurried off in her wake.

I waited until they were gone before I lifted my cloak and took a tentative sniff. Ew. Oh yeah, that was rank. I smelled of the dead thing in the basement. A trip to my dorm was definitely needed before I caught up with Kelsey and Sam in the main hall. On the plus side, at least now I knew where I was.

With a sigh, I hoisted my bag further onto my shoulder, and took the second corridor on the right.

*

By the time I was cleaned up and no longer smelled like something had crawled inside my skin and died, lunch was pretty much over. I caught up with Kelsey and Sam on their way out of the main hall.

"Lyssa, there you are! We were worried about you, are you okay? What Professor Atherton did was *totally* unfair, I think you should complain to Professor Talendale about it. He's always so much harder on us than on the Air students, and everyone can see he's picking on you... What's that smell?"

When Kelsey paused to take a breath, I waved hi to them both and answered her question.

"I'm fine. It's fine. I don't care what Atherton thinks about me."

They both stared at me like I was crazy – which, truth be told, was a fairly common expression Kelsey took on when talking to me, although Sam not so much.

"What?"

"Lyssa," said Sam, "You do realise that you're going to have to get through his exam to pass this year, right?"

I shrugged with more nonchalance than I felt.

"That's ages away. And you guys can help me practice, right?"

"Of course we will," Sam said, shooting daggers at Kelsey who'd raised a finger and opened her mouth like she was about to remind us all that performing magic out of class was strictly forbidden for first years. She raised both her hands in surrender.

"Fine. But if I get expelled, I'm blaming both of you."

"We won't get expelled," I tell her. "We won't even get caught. There's a decent-size copse of trees out on the grounds, just past the dark lake. I saw the gryffs circling it a couple of days ago. What's wrong?"

I added that last because they were both staring at me with their mouths open, horror-struck.

"That's the Unhallowed Grove."

"Oh, I'm sorry for not knowing the difference between a copse and a grove." I rolled my eyes. "Someone expel me."

"They will if you go there," Kelsey said, placing her hands on her hips. "No-one's allowed out there, not even the third years and the prefects."

"Oh. Well, we'll go somewhere else then."

"Not outside, though," Sam said. "You remember what Talendale said at the start of the year — first years aren't allowed to leave the academy after dark."

Dammit. He was right. As much as I didn't want to fall hopelessly behind on my classes and get held back a year, I couldn't risk my friends getting into serious trouble helping me. But there was one place we could go where we wouldn't be caught.

"I think I might know somewhere. If I can find it again. And if you don't mind bad smells."

Chapter Ten

Despite my best efforts, I never managed to find my way back into the hallways I'd ended up in the day I was looking for the library, and not even Kelsey had any idea where they might be. What we did manage to find, though, was an old storeroom that looked like it hadn't been used in a while. It wasn't big, but it was far enough away from the four common rooms and the classrooms that we weren't likely to be disturbed.

Between classes, homework, and working with Alden, it was hard to find time to practice, but I was determined to prove Felicity and Atherton wrong: I was a good druid, and I deserved to be here.

Of course, that was easier said than done. It was a few weeks before we managed to slip away from the common room without anyone noticing. We put as much purpose in our step as we could, but when we rounded a corner and tried to walk straight past Professor Underwood, his stern gaze brought us to a halt. Underwood was one of those people whose ages are impossible to guess. He could have been thirty, he could have been fifty. His short, dark hair was just starting to earn a few grey strands, and his face a few frown lines. And his eyes... well, I couldn't have said. I'd never quite managed to meet them. Everything about the man reeked of inherent authority. He'd have made a good lawyer. Or a cop.

"Where are you three hurrying off to?" he asked, looking between us and then singling out Kelsey. "I'd have thought you in particular had better things to be doing on a day like this than lurking in corridors."

I stared at my feet and tried frantically to come up with something convincing, but Kelsey beat me to it.

"We were just heading to the library, Professor. We wanted to get some studying done."

He eyed us all for a long moment while I steadfastly avoided his gaze. It would probably have made me look guilty as all hell if every other student in the academy didn't routinely do the same thing.

"Very well," he said after a long pause. "Hurry along, then. I wouldn't want to keep you from your studies."

We scampered out from beneath his attention, and I could feel his eyes on our backs the whole way down the corridor.

"Do you think he's rumbled us?" Sam asked, as we rounded the corner.

"I don't think so," I said, counting five doors along until I found the one we wanted. I glanced around just to be sure, and slipped inside. "He seemed pretty interested in you, though, Kels," I added, clicking the door shut behind us.

She just shrugged and helped Sam drag a cabinet in front of the door, blocking anyone from opening it.

"I have some extra study sessions with him."

"Really?" I shuddered. "Rather you than me."

"Well luckily for you, you've just got us," Sam said, wiping his hands on his trousers. "Right, where do you want to start?"

"How about energy pulses? It'd be *really* nice if I didn't need help to get into the common room. I'm the laughing stock of the whole academy."

"You're not the laughing stock of–" Kelsey caught my look and cut off mid-way through her outrageous lie. "Okay. We'll start with that."

"It's as good a place as any," Sam nodded. He dragged a couple of chairs over and brushed the worst of the dust and grime from them, making them marginally cleaner than the floor. Whenever this room had last been used – by anyone other than us – it was obviously long enough ago that it had been taken off the cleaning schedule. Dust webs hung from the ceiling and the cobbled floor was covered in layers of yellowish grime, and a damp, musty scent hung in the air. There were no windows to open so we'd just have to live with that. It was crammed with old boxes, some stacked on shelving units that reached almost to the ceiling, others just dumped on the floor and pushed up against the walls. I flipped one open and found a pile of aging textbooks. Another held what might have been some sort of dried plant matter... or it might not. In one corner there was a stainless-steel sink with a leaking pipe dripping water onto a box beneath it – probably where the damp smell was coming from.

I wrinkled my nose but took my seat and flipped my hand over, so it was palm up. I tried to focus on the faint tingling sensation that ran over the skin of my hand on the couple of times I'd had any success with this exercise. As usual, my palm stayed almost completely skin coloured, with the faintest splotch of pink – less than what you'd get for high-fiving someone.

"Try harder," Kelsey urged, staring at my hand.

"What do you think I'm doing?" I snapped, as my palm flared the tiniest bit redder, and then faded back to skin colour.

"Felicity's right," Sam said, crossing his arms across his chest. "You're never going to get this."

"What?" I tried to keep the hurt from my voice, and failed. I thought he was supposed to be my friend.

"How could you say that?" Kelsey chastised him. "It's just taking her a little longer. It's not her fault that magic doesn't come naturally to her."

"Uh... thanks?"

"Oh, come on," Sam said, staring at me. "I'm just saying what we're all thinking."

I gritted my teeth as he continued.

"You know what Felicity's telling everyone now, right? She's saying if your dad did come here, it must've been as the caretaker, because you've got less magic than a goblin – and that's the only reason Alden took pity on you and gave you that job."

How dare she? How dare *he*? I got up from my chair and stalked towards him.

"I thought you were my friend! Why are you even wasting your time with me, if I'm such a failure? Maybe you should go and ask Felicity if you can join her little fan club."

"Uh, Lyssa?" He backed away, but I kept closing the gap between us.

"You can all have a good laugh at my expense."

"Lyssa."

"I mean, you're all so superior to me, right?"

"Lyssa!" Kelsey shouted. I snapped my head round to her. "Your hand!"

I looked down at my hand and saw the bright red mark pulsing on my skin. I lifted it up, turning it this way and that. I could actually feel the heat projecting out of it. Sam laughed at the look of amazement on my face.

"When you get angry, you stop doubting yourself."

"So... you didn't mean any of that stuff you said?"

"Of course not. Who the hell knows what Felicity goes round saying? Everyone outside of her own house has stopped listening to her, anyway."

The mark on my palm faded. At least I knew I could summon my magic now – I just had to get so angry that I stopped feeling like a total fraud. Easy. *But you're not a fraud,* a small voice in my head said. *Don't you get it? You really do belong here.*

A slow smile spread across my face. Yeah, I did. I didn't need to convince myself, or anyone else. I'd proved it. And I would prove it again, and again, until everyone stopped questioning me.

"Ahh!"

Kelsey jumped and spun around with a loud squeal. Before I could ask her what was wrong, I saw the huge wet patch on the back of her shirt. Behind her, water was gushing down the aging wall stones, cutting a trail through the grime, spraying out of the aging tap. As I watched, the deluge slowed back to the drip it had been before.

"Too bad there's not a water element around here to pull that out of your clothes," Sam said between laughs.

"Well, how about one of the *fire* elements in this room evaporates it?"

"Oh. Right."

Sam raised his hands and started projecting heat from them. He was so far ahead of me it was crazy. There I'd been, celebrating managing to make a weak pulse, and he was projecting enough heat to evaporate water – without burning up Kelsey and her clothes, mind – and all without looking like it took any sort of effort. So much for belonging here. I might be a druid, but I had to be the worst druid Dragondale had ever seen.

"You've got that look again," Sam said, watching me from the corner of his eye as stream rose from Kelsey's shirt. The wet stain was already half its former size, and shrinking rapidly.

"What look?"

He raised an eyebrow like he wasn't buying my act.

"The one that you get whenever you're questioning yourself."

"Just… let it go," I said irritably, turning away from the pair of them, but not before I caught the look they shared. There were few things that irked me more than pity.

"You know what? I've got to get to work. We should pick this up later."

"But Lyssa, we've barely started," Kelsey said, pushing her hair out of her eyes. "I know it's hard, but you're never going to catch up if you don't practice."

"Later!"

107

I tried to shove the cabinet blocking the door out of the way but the damned thing wouldn't budge. I gritted my teeth and shoved harder. Nothing. Rubbing my forehead, I turned back to my friends, not meeting their eyes.

"Can you help me move this?"

"No."

"Excuse me? I need to get out of this room. Now. We'll practice later, okay?"

"I think we need to talk. We're your friends, Lyssa. You're bottling everything up and it's not good for you, you know that. Let us help you."

"You can help me," I snapped, rounding on Kelsey, "by getting this stupid cabinet out of my way before Alden fires me."

"She's not expecting you for nearly an hour," Sam said, nodding to a clock on the wall. He hopped up and sat on the cabinet.

"Please?"

He shook his head.

"Not until you talk to us."

I pivoted on my heel, paced two steps, then pivoted back again. Opened my mouth, then snapped it closed again. I didn't even know where to begin. I backed against the wall, then let myself slide to the ground, and stared at the space between my feet.

"My whole life I've been the odd one out. The one who didn't quite fit in at school, the one who struggled in classes, wasn't as smart as my little sister, didn't even have the same colour eyes as the rest of my family. Then I find out I'm a druid, and I'm adopted, and I don't have time to even begin dealing with that before I'm thrown into classes at 'The Dragondale academy of Druidic Magic'."

I put on a poor imitation of Rufus's voice, then exhaled slowly and leaned my head back against the wall.

"And I think, 'Hey, maybe you've finally found the place you fit in.' But I haven't. I don't fit in here. I can barely even connect with my power and I'm not like anyone else inside these walls. What if I never find the place I fit in? I'm sick of being an outcast. I just want to belong somewhere. Anywhere."

"That's what this is all about?" Kelsey said, glaring at me. Her hands were balled into fists and she was trembling. I didn't think I'd ever seen her angry – truly angry – before. I frowned, confused, but before I could say anything, she continued, eyes blazing. "Do you think you have the monopoly on being an outcast? Do you think you're the only one who doesn't belong?"

Sam hopped down from the cabinet.

"Hey, Kels, take it easy on her."

"Maybe if you took your head out of your own arse for five minutes, you'd realise that you're not the only one here with problems."

I pushed myself up from the ground, trying to work out why she was so rattled.

"What are you talking about? I don't–"

"You don't understand? Well, there's a surprise. You know, you might be surprised by what you understood if you just paid attention to something other than yourself!"

She shoved the cabinet away from the door and yanked it open. Without another word, she stalked out into the corridor, slamming it shut behind her. I looked at Sam.

"What was that all about?"

"Search me. Do you think we should go after her?"

I shook my head.

"Best give her some space. I'll catch up with her later and grovel as soon as I work out what I did wrong." I paused. "Am I really self-absorbed?"

He held up a hand, palm downward, and wobbled it side to side.

"A little."

I grinned and tossed my bag at him.

"Jerk."

He tossed it back.

"Outcast."

He picked up his own bag and slung it over one shoulder.

"We should probably get going before someone notices we're in here."

I glanced at the clock again and nodded.

"I really do need to get out to the barn. Meet you in the common room later?"

"Sure. Don't think I'm going to let you in again, though. You can do your own pulse from now on."

Chapter Eleven

The gryffs seemed to be particularly ornery that evening – or maybe I was the one in the bad mood. Either way, by the time the third gryff had taken a snap at me – the last one coming within a hair of removing one of my ears – Professor Alden suggested I should finish early. That seemed like a sensible idea, so I headed back to the common room, took the coward's way out and followed another Fire inside, got cleaned up and headed down to the main hall in time for the start of dinner service.

I made my way to the back of the queue, but Sam called my name and waved me over – he was halfway up the queue. I caught up with him and saw Kelsey was there too. I coughed and forced myself to meet her eye.

"Are you– Are things okay between us?" I would have apologised for whatever I'd done to upset her, but I still hadn't worked out what it was.

"I hope so," Kelsey said, looking every bit as awkward as I felt. "I'm sorry. I shouldn't have gone off at you like that. Forgive me?"

"It's already forgotten."

We shuffled a few steps closer to the counter as the queue moved. I wished I could forget it that easily. I wished I knew what the hell I'd done. I mean, sure, I was whining a bit… alright, a lot, but still, it seemed like a bit of an overreaction. But I didn't want to start another fight with her. If she wanted me to let it go, that's exactly what I'd do. We shuffled forwards again.

"So, are we going to… you know," I glanced over my shoulder at the other students nearby and lowered my voice, "meet up again later?"

Kelsey shook her head and quickly looked away.

"I'm sorry, I can't this evening. I've, um, I've got something I need to do."

"Anything we can help with?

"No! I mean, no, thank you, it'll be fine."

I opened my mouth but we'd reached the front of the queue and Kelsey was putting her plate down.

"Evening, Aiden," she said, with a bright smile.

"Good evening, Kelsey, what can I get for you?"

"I'll have a steak, please. Rare. Actually, make it blue. And mash and peas… and onions rings and mushrooms."

"You got it."

He did his thing, and suddenly her plate was piled high with the food. I eyed it enviously. If I ate that much, I'd be the size of a hippogryff. I put my plate on the counter and asked for a small slice of lasagne and a side salad. Sam got a burger and fries, and we headed off to a table in the Fire quarter.

Sharna and Dean, two of the other first years in our history of magic class, were already at the table, pouring over a textbook while they ate.

"Can you believe Professor Godwin is only giving us a week to write this assignment on the goblin wars in the eighth century?" Dean complained as we took our seats. "I mean, who even knows anything about the goblin wars? And who cares?"

"What I can't believe," a voice said from behind us, "is that it's Friday evening, and you're studying. I hear Kevan is having a Halloween party – all elements invited."

Alex put her plate on the table next to mine and pulled out a seat, flicking her dark blonde hair out of her face.

"That beats goblins any day of the week."

"Have you seen how many factions there were?" Dean buried his head in his hands. "It's going to take me all night to get my head round this."

"So you're telling me," Alex said, leaning over the table to look at his text book, "that you're going to pass up a Halloween party, when it's a full moon, in the basement – with no professors there – to learn about Krokt the Sriak?"

"She makes a good argument," Sharna said, flipping the book shut. "We can study tomorrow."

"Are you daft?" Dean stared at her with his mouth open, as if she was, in fact, daft. When she didn't reply, he continued, "Tomorrow's the Itealta game – Fire vs Earth."

"Oh, right. I forgot. We can study Sunday, then."

"Forgot? How could you possibly forget? It's the first game of the season. Hope our team aren't going to be a wreck after your party."

He glared at Alex who just shrugged and tossed her hair again.

"Hey, it's not *my* party. Besides, it's just a training match, no-one takes those things seriously. It's not like it's the real thing. And if they can't play after a little party, do they really deserve to be on the team?"

She swept her eyes round to the rest of us, apparently certain that no-one would waste their time with a practice game when the season proper didn't start until the new year.

"Pretty much the whole academy will be there, from what I hear. Aiden says it's a yearly thing – the professors turn a blind eye, you know, so long as no-one gets killed."

"Uh, do people usually get killed at academy parties?" I asked, with a little tickle of trepidation in my stomach. I *had* been thinking of going – even though I had to be up early the following morning to help get the gyffs ready for the match.

"Oh, not in fifty years or so," Alex said breezily.

"Right."

"So, I'll see you there, right?" she asked, downing the rest of her water and picking up her plate. I glanced over at Kelsey and Sam. Sam shrugged but Kelsey shook her head.

"I've got somewhere else to be. Hey, are you finishing that?"

She nodded at Alex's plate, which had an untouched sausage swimming in gravy.

"Knock yourself out," she said, putting her plate on top of Kelsey's empty one. "And you don't know what you're missing. The parties are the only reason I came to Dragondale. Well, that, and I didn't want to be bound. Catch you later."

Several hours later, I was hunting through Kelsey's wardrobe, looking for a top I could wear to the party – since I had no mundane clothing other than what I'd turned up wearing, Kelsey had generously offered me full rein of her wardrobe for the evening. Luckily, we were about the same size. She was a little broader across the shoulders than me, but not enough that it would notice if I wore something sleeveless. I was seriously going to have to find a way to convince the prefects to let me through to Fantail Market now that I had some money. There's only so far you can get on a single pair of jeans and a t-shirt.

I pulled out a red skimpy top and turned to Kelsey, who was sitting cross-legged on her bed, fidgeting.

"Are you sure you don't want to come? You'd look killer in this."

She shook her head.

"You're quiet this evening," I said, as I kept rooting through the rack of clothes.

She shot me a shy smile and managed to still her hands for a moment.

"Sorry, I'm just a little distracted."

"Anything to do with whatever you're up to this evening? Hey, you're not meeting a guy, are you?" I rounded on her, eyebrow raised. "Because I'm your best friend, I deserve the juicy gossip. My love life sucks: I need to live vicariously through yours."

She just smiled and shook her head again.

"You should wear the red one. It'll look great on you, you've got just the right figure for it."

And if she still sounded just a little distracted, I pretended not to notice. Some things just weren't my business. She'd tell me about her mysterious boyfriend when she felt ready. She obviously had her reasons for keeping it quiet. Maybe he was a third year. Maybe he was a professor. My eyes widened as I looked at my innocent friend, twisting her hands in her lap. Okay, probably not a professor, but still. If she wanted to keep it to herself, she could. And I was absolutely not going to pry. For now.

I pulled the red top over my head – she was right, it was more than a little flattering, even if I was getting a little sick of red after two months at the academy. I knew it looked good, because by the time I'd finished sorting my hair and emerged into the Fire common room, a couple of jaws hit the floor. Sam got up from the sofa he'd been waiting on, dressed in a pair of jeans and a shirt that was buttoned halfway. He held his arm out to me like an old English gent. I snorted.

"In your dreams, Devlin."

He laughed, and we ducked out of the common room, pausing long enough to grab our cloaks – it was cold in some of the older corridors. A couple of others came with us, and as a group we made our way down to the dungeons. I hadn't been there before – this place was massive and I doubted I'd even seen a quarter of it yet – but some of the second and third years with us knew the way. The further we went, the darker the corridors got, until we reached some where the ancient fire balls hanging in the corners were dull and flickering, and casting more shadow than light. Derek – a third year boy with long, dark hair tied back in a bun – did something I couldn't quite make out with his hands, and then a fireball sprung into existence between them. He gestured and it floated out in front of us, illuminating our way. The joys of not being under the first-year magic restriction. And having some sort of control of your powers, of course — that must be nice.

As we got closer, it became easier to find where we were going — we just had to follow the sound of the music booming from ahead until we reached the dungeon, where the bass was so powerful I could feel it through my legs as I moved. Through the open door we could see the bare walls covered in cobwebs, which may have been decoration but I suspected it just hadn't been cleaned down here in a really long time. Tiny fireballs hung in the corners, giving off just enough light to let us see the writhing mass of bodies. Practically the whole academy had to be here. I couldn't believe Kelsey was missing this. I mean, boyfriend or not, surely she wouldn't want to miss her first real party?

As the others made their way through the throng, I held back.

"What's up?" Sam shouted in my ear above the roaring tones of a band whose name I didn't know.

"I'm going to find Kelsey," I shouted back.

"Are you sure?"

"She shouldn't miss this!"

Sam nodded his agreement.

"Want me to come?"

"Don't worry," I shouted with a shake of my head. "I won't be long."

I slipped out, leaving him to work his way to the makeshift bar. The booming of the music faded to a distant thrumming as I moved further from the dungeon, tracing my footsteps back through the long corridors and trying to remember which turns we'd made.

I knew I was on the right track because each fireball I passed was a little brighter than the one before, signalling that I was nearing the more commonly used parts of the castle. I was obviously getting better at this: I'd only made one wrong turn so far. Ahead, I recognised an Earth and Fire tapestry hanging on the clean walls, and knew I was approaching the hallway that branched off towards our common rooms. I was about to turn right, towards the Fire dorms, when I saw a figure lurking to my left. I recognised the short, dark skinned Earth element – she was a first year, too. Elaine, I thought her name was. Or Elanor. Something like that.

"The party's that way," I said, gesturing with a thumb over my shoulder. She nodded and chewed her lip.

"I'm heading back there in a minute," I told her. "I just want to see if Kelsey has changed her mind. You can come with us, if you're worried about getting lost."

She looked down at her feet as she spoke.

"Kelsey isn't here."

"Huh? She was here, like, half an hour ago."

The Earth element shook her head, sending braided hair flying around her face.

"I saw her leaving."

"Leaving? Leaving where?"

"The castle."

I frowned. That didn't make sense. First years were banned from leaving the castle after dark, and Kelsey was paranoid about being expelled. There was no way she'd venture out onto the grounds in the middle of the night.

"Are you sure? Maybe she was just heading somewhere else, near the entrance."

She shook her head again, adamant this time.

"I... I followed her." I narrowed my eyes and she said quickly, "I thought she might be going to the party. But she wasn't. She went outside. Towards the Unhallowed Grove."

My mouth hung open. That was the grove that was off limits to everyone, even the prefects, and especially to first years.

"You're mistaken. It must have been someone else, or—"

I remembered how restless Kelsey had been while I was preoccupied with choosing my clothes. Because she was planning on breaking some serious rules? But she'd be at risk of being kicked out and bound, she had to have known that. No guy was worth that. And if Elaine had seen her, anyone else might have, too. Oh, God, she was going to get herself expelled.

"I've got to go. Thanks, Elaine."

I turned and darted back along the corridor. Behind me, the Earth mumbled something that might have been 'Elanor.'

The hallways were deserted, probably thanks to all the students being at the party, and all the professors pretending that they weren't. I pounded along them. Maybe I could catch up with Kelsey before she reached the grove. Who knew what lurked in there? Something bad if everyone was banned from going anywhere near it. Maybe even something dangerous. Suddenly getting expelled was the last thing on my mind. Kelsey could get herself killed.

Chapter Twelve

I didn't slow down until I neared the entrance hall, and then I crept as quickly as I could, peering into the shadows and straining my ears for any sign that I might not be alone. If a professor found me now, I'd never be able to explain what was going on without getting us both in serious trouble. And if I saved Kelsey's life, only to get her expelled, she'd kill me herself.

As I approached the large oaken doors, they swung slowly open, unveiling the dark grounds ahead. I threw one last look over my shoulder, and slipped through, out into the cold night air. It was just as well I was still clinging to my cloak. I took a moment to swing it over my shoulders. The grove was about as far away from the castle as you could get. Kelsey probably hadn't reached it yet. If I ran, maybe I could catch up with her before she got there. As long as she hadn't been running herself. I set off at a fast jog – I was fit, but there was absolutely no way I could sprint that far. As I got further from the castle, the ground became uneven. The earth was damp underfoot, sending me slipping and sliding each time I followed a turn in the trail. I was breathing heavily, head down watching where I put each foot, when I heard it.

A snort. Loud.

I skidded to a halt and pivoted my head round, searching the darkness. Movement to my right caught my eye and I twisted round to face it, taking in the darker patch in the darkness – the massive darker patch. I started to back away, not taking my eyes from the creature. Yellow eyes blinked at me and it stretched its neck. The clouds rolled back from the moon and its light glinted on–

"Stormclaw!"

I gasped in relief, and he snorted softly, stretching out his massive wings.

"I thought you were Ares," I told him. He trotted towards me, pushing his beaked head out to nudge me.

"Sorry, fella, I don't have any fish."

He tilted his head, squinting at me with one bird-like eye, then butted me again, pushing me back a step.

"Not now, Stormclaw. Kelsey's in trouble."

He snorted again, louder this time, and butted me a third time. Before I could say anything, he bent his front knees, lowering himself right to the ground – the position I'd seen other gryffs take to allow their riders to mount.

"You've got to be kidding me," I breathed. He just blinked in response, keeping his front end low. "You know I can't ride."

And even if I could ride, I'd seen the other riders – they used saddles. And head collars. And they wore safety equipment while they were learning. And Professor Alden said *no-one* could ride Stormclaw.

And if I didn't do it, Kelsey was going to land herself in serious trouble.

I let out a long breath, gritted my teeth, and stepped closer.

"I'm trusting you," I told the gryff. He stayed perfectly still, as if he could sense the anxiety churning in my gut. There was a reason I'd never ridden before – like it was absolutely insane. Humans were not meant to ride on the backs of half horse, half eagles.

I closed the gap between us, and tried to work out how I was supposed to get on his back without any stirrups or mounting blocks. Apparently aware of my dilemma, he lifted one clawed foot, forming a platform in front of his wing.

"Right. Of course."

There was no other way to beat Kelsey to the grove. I had to do this.

"We're just going to run, right? On the ground." I said to the gryff as I climbed onto his leg then scrambled onto his back. I was absolutely certain I imagined the amused glint in his eye.

I sat astride his shoulders, one leg hanging down on either side of his neck. Without a head collar and reins there was nothing to grab hold of, and I didn't think he'd appreciate me grabbing a fistful of his feathers – I'd accidentally plucked one from one of the other gryffs, and I knew how badly that ended.

He took off at a lope before I could work out what to do, leaving me clinging to him with my knees and bouncing against him with every step he took. He rustled his wings, but otherwise made no objection, though it had to be as uncomfortable for him as it was for me – and I was certain if he picked up pace or took a sharp turn, I'd be thrown off his back. We were going fast enough that any sort of fall was going to break my all-too-human bones, and leave me stuck in the hospital wing, trying to explain what I was doing on the grounds after dark. And it would be worse for Kelsey, and whatever trouble she'd walked into. Instinctively, I took a deep breath and released it slowly, then loosened the death grip I'd made with my knees, wrapped my lower leg around him instead, and tried to relax my hips. Immediately I felt myself moving with him, rather than being jolted around by his odd stride. My hands hung by my sides, clenched into fists as I fought the instinct the grip something – anything – to keep me on board the massive animal.

Trees rushed by on either side of us as we raced away from the castle, and somehow I stayed astride the massive beast. A branch hung low over the track ahead. I leaned forward, ducking low against Stormclaw's neck, and narrowly avoided being catapulted back. For a full thirty seconds I had myself convinced that he would listen to me, and we would just run to the Unhallowed Grove. Then another branch overlapped the track – this time level with his shoulders. He took a sideways leap to dodge it, almost tossing me into the dirt. I let out a squeal of panic, and then sucked in another breath. Behind me, I felt feathers brush the back of my legs. Dread welled in the pit of my stomach and I risked a look over my shoulder, and blanched.

"No, Stormclaw, don't!"

But he didn't listen. His wings were already stretched out, the speed of our gallop running the wind through his flight feathers. He flapped them twice with lazy grace, and we lifted a few inches from the ground. Another flap, and we rose higher, and then higher still. I glanced down over his shoulder to the ground and my stomach lurched. We were already high above the trees. The galloping motion stopped and his gait became smooth as his wings propelled us through the air. Every few seconds he flapped them, raising his shoulders – and me on them – and then the movement would flatten out again, like a boat being lifted by a gentle current. It felt… magical.

Laughter bubbled up through my lips. We were flying, outlined high above the night sky, the full round moon so big I could almost reach out and touch it, and I had never felt so completely free. Graceful. Perched on his shoulders as he bore me faster though the night air so that it chilled my cheeks and nose. The sound of my laughter was ripped from my lips and left far behind us, and I could hear nothing but the beating of wings and the whoosh of air passing us. I could fly like this forever, far above all my troubles, far above the castle where I was an outcast, far above Felicity and her taunts, far above– Far above Kelsey and whatever dangers she faced.

I set my jaw and fixed my eyes on the grove in the distance. Almost as if he could sense my change in mood, Stormclaw beat his wings faster, then pinned them closer behind him, propelling us through the air more quickly, more determined. We had to get to the grove before she was hurt.

"Come on!" I urged him, crouching low over his neck. He pushed on again until the ground was a blur and I'd have been screaming in terror if I wasn't so focused on getting to the grove. The faster we moved, the harder it became to stay relaxed and fight the little voice that told me I was going to plummet to my death. I forced each breath in and out of my lungs, and tried to unclench my hands that had balled into fists again. It wasn't going to happen. I gave it up for a bad job, instead working on keeping my lower legs round his shoulders and resting on his chest. Soon, impossibly soon, the grove loomed ahead of us. Stormclaw dipped his shoulders and the trees came rushing up towards us, and I knew without a shred of a doubt that we were going to thud into the ground and I would be thrown clear over the gryff's shoulders. A scream burned its way up my throat but I bit down on my lip, hard, trapping it in my mouth. The last thing I wanted to do was disrupt the creature's focus while we were plummeting towards the ground. His wings flared out wide on either side of me and stayed out, slowing our descent. At the last moment I leaned back. His front legs hit the ground with a thud, tossing me forward, and a split second later, his back legs touched down, tossing me back again. He slowed to a trot, then a few strides later a walk, and then came to a complete stop, inches from the first tree.

I let out a shaky laugh, counted my limbs and found them all intact, then gave the beast a heavy pat on his shoulder. He snorted and tossed his head, then crouched low on his forelimbs.

"Yeah, good idea."

I slid down from his back and landed on shaking legs which gave way the second they touched the ground. The gryff butted his massive shoulder against me, propping me up before I hit the deck. I reached a hand out to him for support, and found he wasn't even breathing heavily.

"Guess that's everyday stuff for you, huh?"

He made his thrumming noise and curled his head into me. I gave him a scratch between the eyes, then peered into thicket. It was gloomy beyond the treeline, dark enough that once inside I wouldn't be able to see more than an arm's length in front of me.

"Come on, then," I said, and stepped forward. As I moved into the shadow of the first tree, there was a loud snort from behind me. Stormclaw tossed his head and snorted again, scraping at the ground with a talon.

"Guess I'm on my own."

He jostled his wings and backed up restlessly. I crossed back to him and rubbed my hand along his beak.

"Good boy. Go on, go home."

Without another backward glance, I stepped into the grove. Immediately, the darkness swarmed around me, like a living, breathing creature that was determined to smother me. Low hanging branches snatched at my clothing as I passed, and long vines as thick as my wrist tried to entangle me. It was impossible to move any faster than a walk, and even then, the thick roots of the trees caught my feet and threatened to send me tumbling to the ground.

More than once, I heard something moving in the leaves. Just the wind. It was just the wind. There was nothing there. The hairs on the back of my neck stood on end as I worked my way through the damp woods, keeping to the narrow animal track as best I could. Something clung to my face and I barely bit back a scream. A cobweb. It was only a cobweb. A thought occurred to me and I frantically brushed my hands over my face, my hair, my shoulders. Where there were cobwebs, there were spiders. I hated spiders, creepy little things with too many legs and eyes, and their hairy black bodies, and– I shuddered, then forced the image from my mind. There were worse things in the grove than spiders. Not creepier, but worse.

By now it was so dark that I had to walk with one hand stretched out in front of me, protecting my face from vines, low-hanging branches, and yes, cobwebs. More than once I thought a damp vine under my hand moved, and was glad the moon was hidden by the clouds and the canopy. Some things it was better not to see.

How the hell was I supposed to find Kelsey out here? What was she even doing creeping around this place in the dead of the night? I didn't care who her boyfriend was, there just had to be better places to meet. No guy was worth getting killed for. Or getting spiders in your hair. I could blunder around all night and not find her – assuming I lived that long. I didn't dare call out to her, lest I alerted whatever lived here to my presence, and some deep-seated dread told me exactly how much of a bad idea that would be.

High above me, something rustled in the canopy. I looked up just in time to see a dark shape outlined against the sky, leaping from one tree to the next. I really hoped it was a monkey. Somehow, I didn't think it was. I froze in place, not even daring to draw breath, but it moved on without paying any attention to me.

I pressed on carefully, slowing my progress to little more than a crawl. Far to my left I caught a sound of the very edge of my hearing, like a distant gurgling or... splashing? A stream, perhaps. Weird. I'd seen this place from the air, and there weren't any streams running in or out of here. No matter. Running water had to lead somewhere, and it beat wandering around in circles in the dark. I changed my course and worked my way towards it. With each step the sound became more distinct until I could I hear the water rushing over rocks and foliage in its bed. I came on it all of a sudden: one moment I was pushing through a thick wall of greenery, the next I was on the riverbank with clear sky above me. The stream itself was narrow, littered with rocks and broken branches in the inky-black water that seemed to babble over them in a leisurely fashion. Every now and then there was a silver-yellow glint in the water as the moon peeked from behind the clouds, and then vanished again.

I eyed the gap between the banks. I could probably clear it with a jump if I took a run up, but this side was a good as any. I looked left and then right, and decided to follow it downstream, since that was closest to the direction I'd been moving in before I heard it. I didn't want to end up back where I started without having found Kelsey.

I tracked the stream from its bank, taking care with my footing in the damp mud. When I saved Kelsey's backside, she was going to owe me some new footwear. Then the moon emerged again, and footwear became the least of my worries. Sunk into the mud was a massive pawprint, edged with smaller, deep grooves that only could have come from a set of razor-sharp claws. My feet rooted themselves to the ground and I looked around me frantically. I couldn't see any sign of the beast that had left them, but that didn't mean it wasn't out there, watching me from the treeline. A shudder ran the length of my spine, but I forced myself to keep moving. If you act like prey, you are prey, someone had once told me. Of course, they were talking about schoolyard bullies, not man-eating monsters living in magical groves. I wasn't entirely convinced the same principles applied out here. But I had nothing to gain from standing around, waiting for it to happen. The sooner I found Kelsey, the sooner we could both get out of here, and back to the safety of the castle, hopefully without being expelled, eaten, or both.

I ducked low to avoid a broken branch hanging in the narrow track in front of me, and as I did, my foot snagged in a tree root. My arms windmilled frantically, but the wet mud slipped and slid underfoot and I hit the ground with a heavy thud, knocking the wind out of me. For a moment I laid there in the mud, trying to catch my breath, then I stretched out my leg tentatively, and flexed my ankle. It was throbbing, but I didn't think anything was broken, thank God. The thought of being stuck out here, unable to run, was more than I could bear. Another shudder ran through me, and I started to push myself up from the mud. And froze. Across the stream, a pair of yellow eyes were watching me. My breath caught in my throat and my limbs all locked up. The eyes were round and bright, like a wolf's... only bigger. I'd seen wolves at the zoo, and these eyes were too high up. Much too high. Whatever this was, it would dwarf a wolf. And it was way too interested in me.

If you act like prey, you are prey.

I took a slow, shuddering breath, and forced myself upright, gripping a tree to help me get my balance. Pain lanced through my ankle as soon as I put pressure on it, and I shifted my weight onto the other side. Running was officially out. Walking seemed unlikely, without something to support my weight.

Across the stream, the eyes tilted, like the creature was cocking its head as it assessed me.

"Get out of here!" I screamed at it with as much anger as I could muster, hoping my voice would scare it away. But whatever it was, it wasn't afraid of humans. It stalked closer, emerging from the treeline, giving me my first look of its wet, pointed muzzle, furry face, and large triangular ears. It *was* a wolf. Only, more like a wolf on steroids. This thing was massive, the muscles on its shoulder so pronounced I could make them out from here. It curled its lips back and the moonlight glinted on a row of razor-sharp teeth, tipped in red. Its paws were bigger than my hands, and it had to be nearly as tall as I was. Its shaggy coat was a reddish-brown and slicked flat with mud. I took a step back before I could stop myself, bumping into the tree behind me, and still the creature stalked forwards. A low growl erupted from its throat as it reached the edge of the stream, and sank back on its haunches, preparing to jump. As soon as it reached my side, I was dead. I had no weapons, I couldn't run, and it wasn't afraid of me. Those teeth would grab hold of me, sink into my flesh... I whimpered in terror and threw up my hands. The stream rushed furiously in sympathy, and the creature sprung.

A surge of anger ran through me. Everything I'd been through, everything I'd overcome, and I was going to die out here at the whim of this feral beast – what the hell was it even doing in a school anyway? What sort of moron would let something like this roam free and not tell anyone? A tingle started up in my hands. *Of course!* My powers. It wasn't afraid of me, but maybe it was scared of fire. It was the only hope I had.

I channelled all my fury into my hands, reminding myself of every cutting insult Felicity had thrown at me, every sneer and snigger, every failed class and every time Atherton had kicked me out for no reason. My hand flared bright red, illuminating the trees around us, and the creature skidded to a halt, sinking back and fixing its yellow eyes on my hands.

My heart leapt – it was working. Relief flooded through me, and then the light in my palm faltered. The creature cocked its massive head again, as though contemplating me. I gritted my teeth and pictured this… thing towering over Kelsey. Whose blood was on its face? If it had hurt her, I *would* find a way to kill it. Fury rushed through me and my blood pounded in my ears. My hand flared so strongly that I could feel the heat it was giving off. The creature whined and backed off a step.

"Yeah, damned right you better run," I told it through clenched teeth. "You come anywhere near me or Kelsey and I'll kill you."

It whined and backed up another step, sinking low on its haunches. I limped forward, still aiming my blinding light at the giant wolf.

"I sure as hell hope Kels gave you a taste of this," I told the animal. It whined again, as though it could understand me. I paused. The gryffs seemed to understand at least some of what I was saying, too. Maybe this creature had some grasp of human speech. Maybe all magical creatures did. And there was no way this beast was anything but magical – nothing naturally occurring could be that big.

"Kelsey would have known that," I said, as much to myself as the creature, and it whined a third time. Not when I finished speaking, but when I started. When I said… No, that was crazy. And yet…

"Kelsey."

Another whine slipped from its bloodied muzzle. It recognised her name. I lowered my hand a fraction, but it made no move to get up or advance on me. Emboldened, I dropped my hand the rest of the way to my side and looked at the panting beast. It was lying in the mud, twitching. Its movements became more frantic with each passing second. As I watched, it gnashed it fangs at its own legs, like it was in agony. Had I done that? My stomach clenched in sympathy, all thought of the creature's earlier behaviour driven from my mind, and the dull fire in my hand extinguished itself. This was a sentient animal, and it was obviously in a lot of pain. A howl escaped its mouth and died quickly to a whimper. I could make out the bones moving beneath its fur coat, and then the fur itself seemed to grow thinner, sparser. I frowned as I watched, staring at its face as its muzzle... shortened. I had no idea what was going on, if it was dying, if something was killing it. If *I* was killing it.

I dropped into the mud beside it, but out of range of its wildly flailing limbs and gnashing teeth, looking frantically around for something I could use to help the animal, but I didn't even know what was wrong, much less how I could help. I turned back to the beast... but it wasn't a beast anymore. Lying in the mud, shivering, was a human girl. One I knew well. Kelsey.

Chapter Thirteen

I stared at my best friend in shock. It was a long moment before I regained the use of my mouth.

"Kelsey? What the hell is going on?"

She refused to meet my eye, and when my mind caught up with my eyes, I realised she was completely naked. Hence the shivering. Right. I yanked my cloak off my shoulders and laid it over her.

"Are you okay?"

She gripped the cloak with a trembling hand and wrapped it around herself. After a moment, she gave a shaky nod, then shook her head.

"What's wrong?"

"What's wrong?" The anger in her voice caught me off-guard, but not as much as the devastation in her eyes. She pushed herself to her feet. "Look at me! Do you know what I am? Do you know what I could have done to you? What are you even doing out here? Lyssa, I could have killed you!"

"I… I don't…" I had no idea what to say. Safe to say this wasn't the reaction I'd been expecting. "I came out here to save you," I blurted.

She barked a harsh laugh.

"Save me? From what? I'm the most dangerous thing in this grove."

I looked the skinny, lanky girl up and down, but I knew that wasn't what she was talking about. After a moment, I forced the question from my mouth.

"What are you?"

"I'm a shifter. A werewolf, if you want to be exact." She smiled bitterly. "A half-breed."

"A half-breed?"

"Half shifter, half druid. An outcast in both societies."

Her words thudded home like a punch to the gut. No wonder she'd lost it when I was whining on and on about being an outcast just because I struggled with my magic. I was still a human, still just an ordinary druid. Not Kelsey. She was something else.

She leaned back against a tree and refused to meet my eye.

"Unions between shifters and druids aren't forbidden, but they're strongly discouraged. It weakens the shifter bloodline, and some people believe the shifter corrupts the druid's magic. Shifters don't have magic, not in the same way druids do. The two sides aren't completely incompatible, but they don't exactly work in harmony with each other. Some say a half-breed is incapable of possessing the strength and the control of a full shifter, and unable to wield an element as well as pureblood druid."

I did something then that neither of us expected. I snorted with laughter. Kelsey scowled at me, but I saw hurt and anger vying for control in her eyes.

"I'm glad you find it so amusing," she said, stiffly.

"I'm sorry. It's just, that's the most ridiculous thing I've ever heard. I don't know much about, uh, shifters, but you just turned back into a human instead of shredding me into confetti. And as for wielding your element, you're in the top quarter of every single one of our classes. You're the most kickass half-breed I've ever met."

"I'm the *only* half-breed you've ever met," she said, but a smile was tugging at the corners of her mouth. "You really came out here to save me?"

"Of course I did. That Elanor girl saw you come out here, and I thought you were going to get yourself killed. Of course, that was before you went all Jacob Black on me."

She rolled her eyes at me, then raised an eyebrow.

"You do realise you could have been killed? Or worse, expelled."

"Oh, please. You love me too much to hurt me."

"Yeah, right. It was my decent halter top I didn't want to hurt."

We both chuckled, and what started as a giggle was soon a bout of uncontrollable laughter as adrenaline and relief caught up with us. The smile faded from my lips as I asked,

"Speaking of getting expelled, do the professors know you're out here?"

"Why do you think the Unhallowed Grove is off limits? I'm still learning to control myself. I can prevent myself shifting any day of the month, except for the full moon. But the professors could hardly ban everyone from the grove just when the moon is full, not without telling everyone there's a half-breed in the academy. And trust me, being the first half-breed in nearly a hundred years is hard enough, without the entire academy knowing."

No wonder she'd been fidgety, and anxious to get rid of me. I dreaded to think what would have happened if she'd shifted in the castle, with people around. A thought occurred to me as her words ran through my mind, and I frowned up at the sky.

"The moon's full now, how come you managed to change back?"

She shrugged and tucked a strand of hair behind one ear.

"I don't know. It's the first time I've managed it. I must really love… that top."

"Well, it's a nice top," I agreed with a nod. "But I'm afraid it got a little grubby on the way out here. Between scrambling through the trees and riding the hippogryff."

"Excuse me?" Her face seemed a shade paler in the moonlight. I grinned.

"I'll tell you all about it later." I shifted my weight, then winced as I put pressure on my ankle. Definitely twisted.

"We should get back to the castle before we get expelled, or you're going to wish I'd gone wolf on you."

"Yeah, that's probably a good idea. Hey, can I lean on your shoulder?"

I hobbled awkwardly through the grove, with Kelsey propping me up. The journey back was much easier than the one out here, despite the pain in my ankle. It seemed Kelsey knew every inch of the grove and steered us onto the widest trails. Her night vision was much better than mine, too. Something to do with her shifter half, she told me. But there were still plenty of noises to keep me on edge, and even her eyes couldn't penetrate deep into the grove's shadowy depths.

"So," I clarified, with forced levity in my voice, "If something tries to eat us, you can change back into your wolf form, right?"

She grimaced.

"Shifting is hard. I can't really turn it on and off at will yet."

"So... no wolf?"

"I thought I was the most kickass half-breed you'd ever met?"

"Well, yeah, but you're also the *least* kickass half-breed I've ever met, and I think there are monkeys in the trees."

"Those aren't monkeys," she said grimly, with a glance up at the canopy. "If you see one, stay away from it."

I didn't bother to point out that I was in no hurry to scale the eerie-looking trees in search of the not-monkeys that probably – like everything else in this place – wanted to eat me.

My nerves were stretched so tight that I almost jumped right out of my skin when a loud sniff came from beside me.

"What? What is it?" I asked Kelsey, catching a glimpse of her flared nostrils beneath a stray moonbeam filtering through the trees. Her face was creased in concentration.

"A... I don't know. I thought I smelled something. Something... bad. It's probably nothing."

We pressed on in silence until she froze again. This time, I smelled it, too. A vile, rotting, dead smell. A smell that made all the hairs on the back of my neck stand on end, and made my instincts scream at me to run. I trembled against Kelsey, then tried to pass it off as a shiver. She wasn't trembling. Her eyes were fixed on the trees to our left, and she was completely rigid.

"Come on, let's get out of here," I said, giving her arm a gentle tug. "How much further?"

She shook herself off and nodded, still staring uneasily into the treeline.

"Not far. Just a few minutes."

We couldn't get out of this place soon enough for my liking. No wonder Stormclaw had refused to set foot inside. He might be a mythological creature, but monsters lived in here. My eyes flitted between the trees on either side of us, in front of us, and the canopy above us as we inched our way along the track. Every now and then I'd look down at the track under our feet, and the moonlight would give me a glimpse of a massive pawprint, or a scrape in the mud from an eight-clawed beast, or the remains of something that had been eaten. I tried not to picture the animals that had left them, but the horrific images invaded my mind – every creature I'd ever seen in my worst nightmares, all of them stalking through the trees, salivating, waiting for the right moment to pounce.

Something rustled in the trees above and a pair of amber eyes paused on us as the dark shape leapt from one side of the track to the other. I stared for longer than I should, then caught myself and quickly jerked my eyes to the track in front of me. Something moved. Moonlight glinted on a pale brown hide, turning the tips of each hair silver, and giving the barest hint of the muscles beneath them before they vanished back into the trees. I froze, breath catching in my throat as I searched the trees left and right, looking for the predator.

"Where did it go?" I whispered to Kelsey, gripping her hand. My voice tremored, and my legs shook under me.

"I don't know," she whispered back. "Keep moving."

I stumbled a little as she lurched forward, and then I caught another flash of the silver-tan hide. A scream burst into my mouth and I clamped a hand over my mouth to stifle it. I watched, horror-struck, as the beast stepped onto the track just a few feet in front of us, revealing a creature the size of a leopard. Its tawny hide was stretched sleek over sinewy muscles, and its fierce head looked like it belonged to a mountain lion. It moved fluidly on six legs, trailing two tails behind it.

"Toby!"

I was so relieved I could have kissed the wampus – if my legs hadn't turned to jelly. He looked terrifying in this form. I'd be running in the opposite direction if I hadn't seen him like it before. No wonder he posed as a cat in the mundane world. He moved towards us, blinking his recognition, and butted my hand with his massive head. Then he leapt easily between the trees and vanished.

"Lyssa!"

The voice came from somewhere in front of us, a distant shout that I could just about make out, followed by another. I recognised the voices.

"Professors Alden and Underwood!" I turned to Kelsey and saw the relief on her face, a mirror of my own. We hurried towards them.

"Over here!" I shouted back, and just a minute later, the four of us met. Underwood gave Kelsey a stunned look.

"Kelsey." He looked between the two of us. "This is... unexpected."

"She knows, sir," Kelsey said. "She saw me in my wolf form. I managed to shift back."

"Impressive. Although," he turned a dark look on me, "I believe you are fully aware of the rules regarding students in the Unhallowed Grove."

I hung my head.

"Sorry, sir. I thought Kelsey was in trouble."

"It was very almost yourself in trouble, Ms Eldridge. Kelsey's training has not yet progressed to the point where it is safe for her to be around others in her feral state. What you did was foolish."

"Though with the best of intentions," Alden said, smoothly. "Perhaps this would be best discussed back inside the castle."

"Indeed," Underwood said, though to which of her statements, I wasn't sure. So, Underwood had been helping Kelsey get control of her shifter powers. I guess that explained why she'd had all those extra study sessions with him.

We followed along by the professors, and it was only a matter of minutes before we reached the edge of the grove. Underwood pulled Kelsey to one side and spoke to her in rapid, hushed tones, leaving me alone with Alden.

"I'm going to be expelled, aren't I?" I asked, staring at my feet. She snorted and I jerked my head up to meet her amused eyes.

"After the way you rode Stormclaw? Not likely. I want you on the Itealta team."

Chapter Fourteen

I don't know how Professor Alden swung it, but at six a.m. the following morning I was out by the barn, ready to serve my first "detention", and feeling like I'd been hit by a truck. It had been the early hours of the morning by the time we made it back to our dorm, and later still when we'd managed to fall asleep. Even then, I kept jerking awake, dreaming of yellow eyes staring at me in the darkness, heralded by the smell of rotting flesh. On the plus side, Madam Leechington, the resident healer, fixed my ankle last night, so at least I wasn't hobbling any more.

If Alden noticed my bleary eyes or the shadows under them, she made no comment. Her face was split in a wide grin as she greeted me, and there was a tall, dark-haired guy by her side, a second year who I recognised vaguely from our common room, and from helping prep his gryff for his training sessions.

"Good morning, Lyssa. This is Logan Walsh, I'm sure you've already met? He's the captain of the Fire team."

He turned a brilliant smile in my direction, and I wasn't so tired that my breath didn't catch in my throat a little.

"Hi, Lyssa. Professor Alden tells me you're a natural."

I shrugged, not trusting myself to speak, lest I squeaked like a hormonal teenager.

"We've got a couple of hours before I need to start getting the team ready for the training match," he continued, "So let's see what you can do."

"I've taken the liberty of bringing Stormclaw in for you," Alden said, "Though I warn you, he's in a foul mood this morning. Not enough sleep, most likely. I've advised Madam Leechington to be on standby."

Great. I didn't get the feeling that a sleep-deprived human and a sleep-deprived gryff were going to be the best combination, but I didn't get the chance to dwell on it because Alden flung the barn door open and said,

"Hurry along now, we haven't got all day. Bring Stormclaw out into the paddock, and then we can get started."

Inside the barn was dark and gloomy: the sun was just starting to emerge but wasn't yet high enough in the sky to filter through the skylights. There was only a single gryff inside, and as I approached him, he jerked his head up and watched me through one beady eye.

"Hey, fella," I said, stretching a hand out cautiously, and hoping he wasn't in a biting kind of mood. "Thanks for your help last night."

He closed the gap between us and butted my hand with his beak, thrumming deep in his throat as I rubbed my hand over it.

"You're not stroppy, are you?" I murmured as I stroked him. "Just misunderstood."

His headcollar was hanging on the wall beside his stable, so I slipped it easily over his head, opened the door and led him out to the paddock, bathed in a red-ish light. Logan nodded his approval, but he'd already seen me handle all of the team's gryffs, so this was no surprise to him – even if Stormclaw had a reputation for being difficult.

"Very good," Alden said briskly. "Mount up, show Logan what you can do, and then we'll pop a saddle on."

I suspected the bruising on her arm had as much to do with the reason she wanted to put off saddling up as wanting to show Logan that I could ride bareback, but I made no comment. I'd ride Stormclaw blindfolded if it meant I wouldn't get kicked out of the academy.

She shut the paddock gate behind us – a formality, since Stormclaw could fly over it without any trouble if he chose – and leaned on the fence beside Logan. I turned my back on them, exhaled slowly, and unclipped the lead rope, keeping one hand through the creature's headcollar. I gave his neck a stroke, and tried not to recall the terrifying sensation of the ground falling away beneath our feet. Assuming, of course, I could get on him at all, given that he wasn't trained to take a knee. Maybe I should have led him over to the fence so I could have climbed it and then jumped on. Too late for that now.

"Hey boy, help me out again?" I murmured in his ear. It twitched back to me, and he snorted softly. I ran a hand over one of his scaly front legs and he snorted again, louder. "Alright, don't eat me."

He rustled his wings, then bent his head round to stare at me through unblinking eyes. Just as I was about to give up and put his lead rope back on, he bent forwards, lowering himself to the ground and lifting one scaled leg to form a platform.

I scrambled on before he could change his mind and climbed onto his back.

"Well, that's different," I heard Logan say, but I couldn't work out if he sounded impressed or derisive. I paid him no attention as I settled in place, patted Stormclaw's neck, and wrapped my lower legs around him.

"Alright boy, let's go."

He took off at a trot that was so bouncy I almost flew right over his head, and then he drifted into a canter, tossing me back and forth for a couple of strides while I reminded my hips and knees how to relax. We followed the fence line at an easy lope, far more leisurely than our breakneck gallop through the night. He seemed to be waiting for some sort of signal from me, but I'd never paid much attention to the Itealta training sessions, seeing as how I'd resolved never to sit on one the back of a flying half-horse, half-eagle – on account of not having a death wish.

"So much for that," I murmured to myself, as we passed the watching faces of Professor Alden and Logan. "Come on, Stormclaw, let's fly!"

He responded to my words immediately, breaking into a gallop, and then flapped his breath-taking wings, lifting us into the air. I lurched forward as his gait changed, but quickly regained my balance and pushed myself back into position, resting my calves on his chest and keeping my hands well out of the way. I looked down and my stomach lurched. I hadn't been able to see everything so clearly last night: had we really been going this fast? Everything beneath us was a blur – a blur that I really, really didn't want to plummet into. I leaned back and gasped in a deep breath, then blew it out slowly. Stormclaw knew what he was doing. He looked after me last night, he wasn't going to dump me now. I hoped.

Alden and Logan's heads were tilted back, eyes shielded against the rising sun as we soared through the sky. I thought I could make out smiles on their faces, but it was hard to be sure from up here.

I leant forward just a fraction, looking for a spot to land.

"Let's go down," I told the gryff, fixing my eyes on the gate. He made a wide circle, bringing us down far more carefully than he had last night, but my stomach didn't unclench until we touched the solid ground, and he brought himself to a stop.

"Not bad," Logan called out, climbing the fence and coming over. "But he was in control, not you."

"I don't know if you noticed," I said, sliding down from the gryff's back, "But he's a bit bigger than me. If he wants to go somewhere, I doubt anything I can do is going to stop him."

Logan laughed.

"You'd be surprised. It's all about your partnership. And training – for both of you. It's one thing to be a passenger, but as an Itealta player, it'll be your job to go after the ball, and you're not going to be able to do that if you can't steer him. That's where your reins and saddle come in."

He must've caught the look on my face, because he said,

"Look, I know maybe three people who could have sat that ride, bareback. You've got a natural rhythm. The tack will just make it easier."

I chewed my lip, not voicing my concerns that Stormclaw might not appreciate me trying to steer him, and might decide he'd prefer I wasn't on his back after all.

The professor appeared a moment later, carrying a saddle and an adapted headcollar to allow for reins to be fitted. The gryff obligingly lowered his head, allowing me to switch his headcollars in exchange for a scratch behind his ear, and then I led him over to the fence so I could reach up onto his back to fit the saddle. It was a little tricky, trying not to fall off the fence while I fitted the saddle to his back, but there weren't any tacking-up steps out here and I didn't get the sense I was supposed to ask for some.

"On you get, then," Alden urged, and I scrambled onto his back and into the saddle. It was made of worn brown leather, with a massive saddle-horn at the front, and a tall ridge at the back, leaving me sitting securely in the middle. The stirrups hung down between them, just in front of his wings – further back than I was used to putting my feet. I took hold of the stirrup leathers and grappled my feet into the irons, trying not to kick Stormclaw in the process. Logan chuckled at my attempts and I shot him a dirty look. He held his hands up in surrender, but the amusement didn't leave his face.

"She's fiery," he said to Alden in a voice I suspect I wasn't supposed to hear. "She'll make a good winger."

With my face still turned away from them, I allowed myself a little grin. I'd never been anyone's pick for sport at school. Finally settled in the saddle, and with my feet in their new, somewhat awkward position, I reached forward to pick up the reins – managing to jab myself in the gut with the saddle horn. I grunted, then smoothed out my face, trying to pretend my stomach wasn't throbbing because of my idiocy.

"Alright, Lyssa," Logan called – they'd made their way back outside the paddock again. "Shorten up your reins. We're just going to get both of you used to the equipment. Stormclaw hasn't been ridden properly in years. It'll feel as odd to him as it does to you. Ask him to walk."

"Uh, walk on, Stormclaw."

He snorted and tossed his head, throwing the reins around in my hands, then backed up three steps and rustled his wings.

"I don't think he likes the reins," I called to Logan, just as Stormclaw threw his head forward, yanking them from my hands and almost pulling me right out of the saddle.

"It's your indecision he doesn't like. Be confident."

I nodded and squared my jaw, then picked the reins back up.

"Let's go, Stormclaw. Walk."

I set my eyes on the far side of the paddock and felt movement under me. The gryff walked forward, his head bobbing with each step. I loosened my elbows, letting myself move with him.

"Yeah, that's it!" Logan shouted from where he was sitting on top of one of the paddock rails. Alden had gone – apparently she'd decided we had it in hand. I wished I had her confidence.

"Steering is easy," Logan told me as we reached him again. "Just squeeze the rein on the side you want to turn to. And I do mean squeeze – if you pull on them, you're going to upset him, and you don't want to do that mid-air, trust me."

Don't yank the rope tied around his face. Got it.

"But most of your steering will be done through body weight, anyway. Look where you want to go, and it'll shift your weight on his back. He can feel that, and he'll respond to it."

Like he did last night when he was taking me to the grove. That seemed much smarter than messing around with reins. I kept my mouth shut and listened to Logan as he carried on instructing me, trying not to zone out with all the details being thrown my way.

"It looks like he's already trained to voice commands to go faster or slower, and he's willing enough to follow them – for you, at least. But you don't want to be shouting your plans out for the other team to hear, so he needs to respond to touch signals, too. Press a hand to his shoulders in front of your saddle to ask him to go faster. Press a hand behind to ask him to slow down. Touch your feet just under his wing to tell him to fly or go higher, and in front of them to ask him to go lower or land. Right, enough talking. Get him moving. I want you to do a ramassage – a pick up. I'm going to throw a ball, you're going to get it and throw it back to me."

It sounded really simple when he put it like that. I pressed a hand against Stormclaw's neck, just hard enough that I could feel the muscle beneath his feathers, and he walked forward. I pressed again and we broke into that awful trot – a third time and we were in the smooth canter.

Logan lobbed the ball into the centre of the paddock. It was about the size of a basketball, but it had metal handles on the top and bottom, and on either side. And it was lying on the floor, a whole lot lower down than I was. I locked eyes onto it and Stormclaw charged at it, responding to the slightest shift in my weight… and then we pelted straight past it, while I was still trying to work out how I was going to get it. I mean, I'd seen the way the players got it, but there was absolutely no way I was going to lean sideways out of the saddle and reach right down to the ground. I circled around and charged it again – and passed it again. I could keep doing this all day, but the ball was hardly about to leap up into my arms. Could I really reach down and scoop it up, without killing myself in the process?

It was Logan's laughter that decided me. I circled around once more at the end of the paddock, and ran at the ball again. This time, I steered just off to the side, so the ball would be on our left – seeing as my right hand was strongest, and that's what was going to be holding me in the saddle. I wrapped my fingers around the saddle horn, then leant my whole body sideways out of the saddle and down to the ground, stretching the fingers of my left hand out as I reached for the ball's metal handles.

And then I fell.

Chapter Fifteen

Between Itealta practice, working for Alden, and my private training sessions with Kelsey and Sam, the next few weeks passed in a blur. I made so many trips to the hospital wing that I could have found my way blindfolded – Logan assured me it was perfectly normal to break a few bones learning to play, but frankly I wasn't convinced. And while it was great that Madam Leechington could mend up broken bones as good as new inside five minutes, it didn't make breaking them in the first place any less painful.

Another full moon passed, and I made no comment when Kelsey disappeared out of our dorm when night started to fall. By the following morning, she'd been back in her bed like nothing had happened, other than the dark circles under her eyes.

The professors piled increasing amounts of work on us with each passing week, and I had no time to think about much else, until Christmas was almost on us. I'd had a letter delivered with the morning post, addressed to me in my mum's neat handwriting. It had taken me a full half hour to bring myself to open it, by which time breakfast was in full swing. It wasn't that I hadn't wanted to hear from my parents, it was just… well, truth be told, I'd been avoiding the whole subject, as if burying my head in the sand would make the whole supposed adoption thing go away. At first, I'd told myself it wasn't the sort of thing you could bring up in a letter, so I would speak to them about it as soon as I got another chance to call home. Then I'd decided it wasn't the sort of thing you could bring up in a phone call, either, and it would be better to speak to them about it when I went home for Christmas. Although I'd been thinking the last few days that maybe it would be best if I waited until *after* Christmas – after all, I didn't want to ruin the festive season for them by bringing up something that was probably just a load of rubbish, anyway.

I tore open the envelope, pushing my half-eaten bacon sandwich in Kelsey's direction absent-mindedly, and pulled the letter out. My eyes quickly scanned the neat script and my mouth popped open.

"I don't believe it!"

"What do you mean you don't believe it?" Sam said between mouthfuls of his cereal. "Of course the first proper match of the season is on the first of January. It's tradition."

"Huh? No, not that. I know about the match, I'm first reserve. I mean this."

I gestured to the letter, but Sam was staring at me with wide eyes.

"You're first reserve on the Fire Itealta squad, and you didn't tell us? That's massive news! Have you stopped falling off yet?"

"What does it say?" Kelsey asked, looking at the sheet in my hands.

"My parents." And despite what Talendale had said, I couldn't bring myself not to think of them as my parents. They'd raised me, what else would they be? "They're going to Paris over Christmas. A second honeymoon, she says. Holly's going to be staying with friends, so there'll be no-one at home."

"I'd invite you to spend Christmas with us, but we're going to stay with," Kelsey threw a glance over her shoulder and lowered her voice, "my mother's family. They're put out enough with just me and my dad."

"You can't spend Christmas alone," Sam said. "I'm staying here at Dragondale this year, why don't you stay as well?"

"Yeah, might as well," I said, but it wasn't the idea of being alone, or the idea of being stuck in the academy at Christmas that was bothering me. I'd really needed to see their faces, see the similarities between us, and prove to myself that this adoption nonsense was just that — nonsense. If the Tilimeuse Tree didn't know who my father was, then it certainly didn't know who he *wasn't*.

"That's settled, then," Kelsey said brightly, stacking our plates. "Let's head over to Elemental 101 before we're late."

I looked around and was surprised to see the hall was almost empty – just a handful of stragglers clearing away their stuff. We hurried to Swann's classroom and got there with about a minute to spare. The three of us dropped into our seats – still in the front row, while Felicity whispered something to Paisley and Cecelia that was probably about me, and I pretended I couldn't hear.

"Everyone stand up," Swann said, rising from her seat behind her desk, which was empty except for a lone candle and a large jug of water. "Come on now, everyone, up, up, up."

There was a loud scraping of chairs as everyone got to their feet and exchanged confused looks.

"We're going to have a little test. Pair up with someone of the opposite element."

Faster than you could say, 'anyone but Felicity', the three of them made their way over to us, nasty smiles on their faces that made me suspect they'd known this was coming. I quickly looked around, but everyone else had hastily found partners, glad not to be paired with Felicity. Swann looked round the room and nodded her approval.

"Excellent. The first pair will come to the front... Sam and Cecelia. Everyone else sit down."

When the scraping of chairs died down again, every eye was on the pair standing at the front.

"Now, Cecelia, come and stand at this end of my desk. And Sam, there, at that end. Good."

Professor Swann lit the candle and took a step back, standing a few feet behind the desk, leaving the two students glaring at each other over the top of the candle.

"When I give the word, Cecelia, you will use your power to attempt to extinguish the flame. Sam, you will use yours to sustain it. Dominant hands only. If the candle remains lit at the end of sixty seconds, you will be the winner. However, should Cecelia manage to blow the candle out within than time, she will be the victor. Do you both understand?"

When they both nodded, Swann looked up at the clock on the wall above her head. As the second hand approached the top, she said,

"Ready... Begin!"

Cecelia threw up a hand, and across the desk, Sam mirrored the action. Both of their hands immediately started to glow. The flame flickered, and for a moment I thought it was going to go out right away, but Sam narrowed his eyes and stared at it, his palm flashing brighter red for a split second, and the flame flared then settled back into place, dancing side to side as it resisted Cecelia's attempt to blow it out with her air magic.

My eyes flicked to the clock on the wall then right back again, not wanting to miss a thing. They were thirty seconds into the challenge, and so far Sam was holding his own, but his jaw was clenched and his brow furrowed. Cecelia's pretty face was screwed up in a scowl and I could see her temper was starting to get the better of her. The hand hanging loosely by her side was balled into a fist and her lips curled back. I risked another look at the clock. Ten seconds.

"Go on, Sam," Dean shouted from the back of the room, and the flame flared again as he redoubled his efforts. Five seconds. His hand wavered in the air, his fingers trembling as he stared at the flame, unblinking. Three seconds. Two. One.

"Finish!"

The flame was still burning as both students lowered their hands.

"Congratulations, Mr Devlin. You may both sit down."

There was loud applause and some whooping from the fire elements as Sam walked back to his seat, grinning. Cecelia joined her friends and the three of them scowled at us.

"Next pairing," Swann said, glancing among the pairs seated near the front. "Kelsey and Paisley."

"Teach her a lesson," Felicity called as they left us.

"You've got this, Kels," I said, and she shot me a worried look in return.

They took their places, and waited for Swann to start them.

"Ready... Begin."

They both flung their hands up, palms immediately glowing yellow and red. Barely ten seconds had passed when the flame flickered and shrank to a third of its size. There came a ragged cheer from the Airs, which silenced as the flame resisted the attempt to extinguish it and was replaced by whoops from the Fire students as the flame grew, edging bigger and bigger by fractions until it reached its original size.

Thirty seconds passed, and the two girls continued to glare at the flame, palms outstretched and glowing. The room was divided by cheers and boos as the rest of the class encouraged and urged them on.

"Go on, Paisley, one more gust!"

"Keep going, Kelsey, not long now!"

The second hand on the clock ticked with painful lethargy, until only ten seconds remained.

"Barely an ember," Felicity sneered. "No wonder she needs all those extra lessons with Underwood. She's almost as bad as Charity."

Kelsey's eyes flicked to the blonde, anger and panic warring in them, for just a split second, but it was long enough. The flame blew out, leaving the merest flicker of smoke rising from the blackened wick, and Paisley grinned triumphantly. The Airs erupted into cheers, while the Fires booed, and called 'Cheat!' loudly, until Swann raised her hands and demanded silence.

"Settle down! The onus is on the competitor to maintain their focus and resist outside distractions. Though," she singled out Felicity and arched a brow, "Unsporting conduct is highly discouraged in my classroom."

Felicity hung her head, but as soon as the professor looked away, she shot Kelsey a snarky look.

"Ignore her," I said, loudly enough for anyone nearby to hear. "She knew they'd never have beaten you in a fair challenge."

"Oh, we'll just see about that," Felicity snarled, anger contorting her pretty face.

"Next pair," the professor called. "Felicity and Lyssa."

She gave me a nasty smile and sauntered up to the desk with a flick of her long hair. No surprise that she looked so confident – I'd gotten better at controlling my elemental power, but I wasn't even close to her level. Kelsey gave me a sympathetic smile, and Sam clapped me on the shoulder, but both of them had the look of someone sending a lamb to the slaughter.

"Thanks for the vote of confidence, guys," I muttered under my breath.

"Professor?" Felicity said, her voice saccharine sweet. "I don't mind challenging someone else if Lyssa is too scared."

"Of you?" I snarled. "Hardly."

I stalked up to the desk, squaring my shoulders and eyeing Felicity over the top of the flame.

"You're the one who should be worried," I told her, forcing a smile onto my face. I wasn't bluffing — I had nothing to lose, everyone already knew I was awful. If she got beaten by me, the outsider, the druid raised by mundanes, she'd be the laughing stock of the entire academy. After everything she'd put me and my friends through, I liked the sound of that.

"Ready... Begin."

Felicity's hand started to move on 'ready', but the professor didn't seem to notice. I flung my hand up a split second later, and already the flame was flickering. Fury flushed through me that she'd dared to cheat so blatantly, with everyone watching, but I channelled the anger and pumped it out of my hand, pouring every bit of heat I could muster through my palm and into the flame, strengthening it against Felicity's attack. I could feel the gust coming out of her palm, blowing cold air around me, but the flame held its own.

From the corner of my eye, I saw Felicity's mouth pressed together in a tight line of anger – she'd thought she would catch me off guard with her early draw, and she certainly didn't expect I would last more than a few seconds against her. I could hear the cheers and shouts of the rest of the class, shouting encouragement to both of us, but I tuned them out and shrank my whole focus to the small, stubborn flame in front of me.

It wasn't until I heard the gasps that I realised something was wrong, and I lifted my eyes a fraction to see a furious Felicity raising both her hands. The class weren't the only ones in uproar: every fibre of my being wanted to punish that dirty, cheating, little airhead. I bared my teeth and glared at the flame. The entire candle fell over, and rolled onto the floor, blown aside by the dual gusts of air from Felicity's hands. The flame didn't go out, protected by my rage.

"That is enough!" Professor Swann shouted, and I immediately dropped my hand. Across the desk, Felicity lowered both of hers, too, but the damage was already done. The candle had blown right into my feet, and the unnaturally hot flame licked at my robe and set it alight. Oh, shit. I couldn't be burned by my own fire, but my clothes certainly could.

A flush of panic turned my veins to ice and I gasped as the professor called for everyone to stay calm – but I was far beyond calm. I looked at the jug of water on the desk, thinking I could grab it and throw it over my clothes before they were completely destroyed, and the next thing I knew, the water was lunging at me, leaving the jug behind, and soaking me right to the skin. The fire died immediately, leaving me standing them in the remains of my smouldering clothing.

"Class dismissed," Professor Swann said, a quiver in her voice. "Study your textbooks in your common rooms. Now! Out. Felicity, see me at the end of the day. Lyssa, I'd like a word."

I paused mid-step. Kelsey and Sam hovered, giving me worried looks as the rest of the students poured out around them. The professor looked at them.

"Off you go, you two. Lyssa will be along shortly."

"What's the matter, Professor?" I asked, as the door swung shut behind them. "Did I do something wrong? I didn't mean for the fire to spread, I haven't learned–"

"No! No, you're not in any trouble," she said, regaining some of her composure. "No-one would have expected a first year to stop the spread of fire. Please, sit."

I sank into the chair she gestured to, trying to read her face but she was giving nothing away. I was forced to wait while she pulled out a chair and sat down. Immediately, she stood up again and started to pace. I wondered if I should say something, but she stopped abruptly and turned to look at me.

"In all my years, I have never seen anything quite like that."

I opened my mouth to ask what she meant, but she raised a hand and I clamped my jaw shut again.

"For how long have you possessed a second elemental power?

"I'm sorry, a what?"

"Don't play games with me, girl!" She slapped a hand down on the desk in front of me and I jumped.

"Professor, I'm not, I–"

"You expect me to believe that you didn't know you were pulling the water from that jug?"

"But, Professor, *you* did that."

She shook her head, then drew in a slow breath.

"No, Lyssa, *you* did that. I've never seen such a thing. I did not even believe it was possible. And to have that level of control without even being aware of it... You must be very powerful indeed."

"What are you saying, Professor?" I said, an uneasy feeling cramping in my stomach.

"That you possess control over opposing elements," she said, holding my eye. "And you are the first in our history to do so."

Chapter Sixteen

I was glad when, just over a week later, the semester finished for Christmas break, and most of the students went home for the festive period. It was a relief to be able to walk the long corridors without whispers following me everywhere I went, and to eat in the hall without dozens of eyes staring at me, wondering what made me so different. I wondered that a lot myself, but even after several meetings with Professor Talendale, we were no closer to getting to the bottom of it. It seemed like the only ones who didn't think I was either the second coming of Merlin, or a total freak, were Kelsey, Sam and Stormclaw. Even Logan had looked at me funny for a while – until I tossed an Itealta ball right in his face, then he kept his eyes where they should be.

Kelsey went home to her family, but not before we'd made time for a little splurging at Fantail Market, where I'd picked out presents for her and Sam, and got myself a few essential supplies - including some brand new robes, which didn't have frayed edges or questionable odours or random burn patches, and text books that weren't full of other people's notes – although I have to admit that some of the notes had been more than a little useful when it came to getting my assignments done. On the other hand, the copious coffee and potion stains had not, and I'd been making do without pages eighty-four through ninety-seven in my Botany textbook since the start of the year. When we got back to the academy, we hugged and parted company, and I tried my best to hide my small pang of jealousy that she was getting to see her family while mine were off on holiday without me, and me and Sam passed a Christmas that was better than I'd expected here at Dragondale.

It was deserted in the library, which was no surprise since it was the day after Christmas: half the students were still celebrating, and the other half were in a food coma. I, myself, would have been happy to be in either camp, but here we were, in the library.

"Remind me why we're in the library on Boxing Day?" I griped.

"Because it's Boxing Day," Sam said, as though that explained everything.

"Right. Of course. I mean, where else would we be on boxing day, except, like, anywhere?"

"Look around," he said, gesturing about the room with an amused look on his face. "What do you see?"

"Books. Lots and lots of books. In the holiday break. You do know what a holiday is, right?"

He rolled his eyes and coughed, tossing an exaggerated nod at the book check-out desk.

"Oh! No staff."

He cupped a hand and tilted his head.

"Is that the sound of the penny dropping?"

I elbowed him in the ribs.

"Ow! Alright, alright. They run an honour system over Christmas and Boxing Day, you have to check the books out yourself."

"And this helps us how?"

He rolled his eyes again and I lifted my elbow. He threw up his hands in mock surrender.

"Don't get aggressive with me just because you're a little slow on the uptake today."

He ducked out of the way of the swat I aimed at his head, and set off through the rows of books.

"There are certain areas of the library that are off limits to us lowly first years. But if there's no-one else here, then there's no-one to stop us looking. If we get caught after the fact–" he paused and plucked a book from the nearest bookcase, pretended to examine in, then put it back again "–we just claim ignorance – something you should be particularly good at."

My hand landed on the back of his head with a satisfying thud, but he carried on, apparently undeterred.

"As far as anyone knows, we're just doing some research for Godwin's assignment. And if we should happen to drift in this direction…"

He trailed off and took a few more steps towards the back of the library. I pulled out a book and flipped it open.

"And what are we going to accidentally find?"

He pulled the book from my hands and shoved it back on the shelf, silencing my protests with a look. I waited. He glanced around the deserted library, and lowered his voice.

"You know, don't you? About Kelsey, I mean."

I froze, watching him closely.

"Know what?" I said, my voice careful.

"Know… where she goes," he said, his voice a match for mine.

"Do you?" I deflected, arching an eyebrow.

"I might have overheard one of her private lessons with Underwood. And I might have accidentally followed her one… full moon."

I breathed out in a long whoosh and leaned back against the bookcase behind me. He knew.

"You were lucky not to be expelled."

"Well, I hear they're offering trespassers in the grove spots on the house Itealta team so I thought I'd give it a go."

"It's the only way you'd get a spot," I taunted him, but my mind was whirring. If he knew she went to the grove, then he knew what she was.

"Thanks. So, we both know, then?"

"You say it," I said, my voice barely a whisper. It wasn't my secret to betray.

"Werewolf."

I swallowed with relief and nodded.

"Werewolf," I whispered back.

We stared at each other in silence for a long moment.

"That still doesn't explain what we're doing here."

"Shapeshifters aren't the only ones who change into animals."

"They're not?"

Sam shook his head, and started walking again, edging towards an alcove at the very back of the room, dark and crammed with dusty books. I glanced at it, then back to Sam.

"Okay, how much attention have you been paying in History of Magic? And Druidic Law?"

I shrugged.

"Some. There was something about goblins."

He sighed in what I assumed was exasperation.

"For someone who was raised outside the magical community, you really could try harder to integrate."

"For someone who got a D on his last Druidic Law assignment, you're awful preachy."

"Ouch. Okay, look, there are three types of magic user, right?"

I nodded. This much I knew.

"Druids, Shifters, and Unclassifieds."

"Right. Shifters being the least magical, able to change forms and not much else. But, they're not the only ones who can do that. There's a highly specialised skill called skin-walking."

"So...." I frowned as I tried to work out where he was going with this. "We could change shape?"

He nodded.

"If we learned the spell, then Kelsey wouldn't have to be alone every month. But," he paused for emphasis. "First and second years are forbidden from even attempting it. We could get in a lot of trouble."

"More trouble than going into the Unhallowed Grove in the middle of the night? Which book do we need?"

Once we got into the restricted section, it only took about ten minutes to find the book. It would have taken less time if we hadn't had to stop every few seconds to make sure no-one was coming into the library.

"Got it?" I hissed, as he pulled yet another tome from the shelf.

"Yeah," he said, dumping it on a small table, and sending a cloud of dust into the air. "Now I've just gotta find the spell."

"Well, do it quickly. This place is creepy."

I trailed a finger along the dusty shelf, looking at some of the titles. 'Soulscraping: Harvesting Dark Power' was emblazoned on one in bright green ink, and another said 'Dream Binding for Mundane Manipulation'. My stomach churned in revulsion. What on earth did anyone need with these books – surely no student of Dragondale was messing with this stuff? Mundanes were protected by law. And somehow, I couldn't picture the diminutive Professor Walmsley discussing the finer points of mind control. On the plus side, it looked like it hadn't been read for a while – a few decades, at least, if the amount of grime on the cover was anything to go by – unlike... I tilted my head sideways to get a good look at the faded grey text. 'The Shadow Grimoire of Necromancy'. Like, zombies and stuff? I shuddered, and moved my finger away, as though death magic might be catching. I so had *not* needed to know that zombies were really a thing. I had enough trouble sleeping as it was. And what next? I mean, I'd been pretty opened-minded about this place, after the initial shock, but how many supernatural surprises was one girl supposed to embrace? I decided right then that if Tinkerbell showed up, I was off, magic be damned.

"Got it!" Sam said, and I almost jumped out of my skin at the sound of his voice, so caught up in my thoughts was I. I chastised myself for being such a coward and went to look over his shoulder. Fair enough, there it was – a page entitled 'Skin Walking' and underneath, details of an incantation and an elemental energy pulse pattern like I'd never seen before.

"Do you really think we can do this?"

"It's pretty advanced," he agreed, squinting at the spell. "Pass me that pen and paper, we'd better make a copy. We can't risk someone finding this book in either of our dorms."

He was right – just holding this book was enough to get us into serious trouble. I chucked him the writing equipment and went back to keeping an eye out. Kinda hard to explain it away as taking a wrong turn when you're in the middle of copying out a forbidden spell.

It took him a few nerve-jangling minutes but he wouldn't be rushed, insisting that if he copied it down wrong we'd be in bigger trouble than anything Professor Dawson would throw at us for being in her restricted section.

"Double check I haven't missed anything," he said, finally setting the pen down. I leaned over his shoulder, checking his notes matched up with the book, and we both pretended not to see that attached warnings. After a long while, during which I tried to blot words like 'immutable-fusation' and 'fragmented-transformation' from my mind, I nodded.

"Looks good to me." *Good* might have been a bit of a stretch, but it was correctly copied, at least. "Where can we try it?"

Five minutes later, we were safely outside the library, and an hour after that, we had barricaded ourselves in the old storage closet we'd been using for my extra-curricular practice sessions, complete with a few supplies we'd grabbed and tossed in my backpack. We'd debated heading out onto the grounds, but we'd never been caught here before, and as far as I could tell, no-one ever visited this place between our sessions.

I dragged a stack of boxes into the middle of the room to serve as a makeshift table, and Sam unrolled the spell onto it. I dumped my bag on the floor and fished out a printed photo, a hand mirror, a bottle of water, and a candle.

"Okay, the mirror goes here," he said, setting the mirror in the middle of the 'table', "and the candle goes here. Then the water opposite it, and the photo, yeah, right there."

By the time we'd fussed around, our hastily constructed altar had a mirror in its centre, and the candle sat furthest away from us, between the mirror and the door. The water was on the other side, nearest to us. The photo went on the left of the mirror, and there was an empty space to its right.

"Okay, who's going to try it first?" Sam said, sounding suddenly uncertain. I took a breath and tried to sound more confident than I felt.

"I'll do it."

"Yeah, great idea. It's only six days until our Itealta game against Air. The team will be thrilled if you're still stuck on all fours."

"Well, all the more motivation for you to fix me, then. Anyway, no-one's getting stuck. Put the spell here."

We put the spell just on the edge of the altar, so it wouldn't interfere with anything. Hopefully. I was starting to think maybe we should have taken a moment to read those warnings. Oh well, no time to panic now. I reached behind my head and plucked out a few hairs.

"Do you think that's enough?" I said, setting them on the altar, opposite the photo of the dog we'd found in the Fire common room. Sam shrugged.

"Gee, thanks for the reassurance," I said, rolling my eyes at him.

"Stalling, much?"

"I am not stalling," I lied. I took a breath and summoned a flame onto the candle wick, pleased that I managed to get it first time. My smile quickly faded – that was the easy part, and it would be the last part that was. I stretched out trembling hands above the hair and the photo and glanced down at the incantation. It was in

Gaelic, but luckily I'd been paying enough attention in that class that I didn't stumble over too many of the words, even if I couldn't have translated half of them. I didn't need to know what they meant, so long as they worked.

I reached the end, then gave two short pulses of heat, taking care not to set the hair or the photo alight. I gave another, longer pulse, then moved my hands to the opposite side of the altar, so the one that had covered the hair covered the photo, and vice versa, and my arms formed a cross directly above the mirror. A quick glance at the spell sheet told me I needed another six pulses of various lengths, then I uncrossed my hands, gave four more pulses, and crossed them again.

I drew a shaking breath, locked eyes with myself in the mirror, and gave one final, long, powerful pulse.

"Cruth-atharraich!"

I kept staring at myself in the mirror for a long moment, then disappointment flooded through me. I was still staring at my own brown, distinctly human eyes. And I hadn't shrunk.

"Dammit, it didn't work. I suppose it was asking a lot to get it right on the first try. Why don't you have a go? Maybe you'll have more luck than me."

I turned around and caught Sam staring, open-mouthed.

"Seriously, have you been staring at my butt this whole time?"

He didn't answer but raised a hand to point.

"What?"

I spun around and caught a flash of movement from the corner of my eye.

"What was that?"

My question was answered when I heard the steady swish-swish-swish of a fluffy tail brushing the cardboard boxes. *My* fluffy tail.

Chapter Seventeen

I t took us three hours to get rid of that damned tail, and by the time we had, neither of us felt much like carrying on that day. We tried the next day, and the day after, and the day after that, but we never had any more successes. Not even tail. Not so much as a hair.

"How is it so hard?" I groaned, after yet another failed attempt and another of our precious days lost.

"Maybe it wasn't such a great idea. This is really advanced magic."

But I couldn't help feeling that if I could ride a hippogryff, and I could control two opposing elements, taking on the form of a dog should be easy. And yet, here we were. I gathered the stuff from the altar and helped Sam stow it away in a box in the corner. We'd try again tomorrow – and as many more days as it took. Even if it took the rest of our time here in Dragondale, we were going to master that damned spell.

"Half of the academy is getting back tomorrow," Sam said, as we checked the coast was clear and slipped out of the room. "They're coming back for the New Year's party, and the Itealta game.

"Don't remind me." I felt like I had a gut full of squirming snakes every time I thought about the match. It was ridiculous, because odds were I wouldn't even play –

they had a full team, and I was just the reserve. Yet the idea of riding in front of half the academy was enough to make me reconsider how smart it was to accept Logan's offer. I'd never even seen a gryff four months ago. Riding one in a match against eight highly experienced players seemed like a bad idea. A really bad idea.

"Hello, earth to Lyssa?"

I blinked Sam back into focus, to see him waving a hand in my face. I swatted it aside.

"What?"

"Are you heading to dinner, or have you got practice?"

I checked the watch on my wrist and cussed in a most unlady-like manner.

"Practice. I've gotta run. Catch you later."

I was panting slightly by the time I got to the paddock and found someone had already tacked up Stormclaw – a brave move, since he was prone to biting anyone who wasn't me. The rest of the team was already mounted, except for one. I glanced over at the chestnut-coloured gryff and tried to remember who usually rode her.

"Sorry," I gasped to Logan, untethering Stormclaw from the fence.

"No problem," he said, and one of the guys behind him rolled his eyes – Logan had a tendency to take it easy on me. "We're still waiting for Keira."

Keira, that was it. The blonde third-year. A quiet girl, she could usually be found out on the grounds, keeping her own company, but she was punctual to a fault. Odd.

"Right, we can't wait any longer," Logan said, wheeling his gryff around. "Keira will have to join in when she gets here."

He touched his heels to his massive, pure white beast, and the heavily muscled animal leapt forward and took to the air. Logan was such a skilled rider that even from here I could barely make out the signals he gave to his gryff, steering him effortlessly through the skies. One by one, the rest of us followed suit, until we were all circling above the paddock.

"Trius manoeuvre," Logan shouted. "Josh."

Josh gave the barest of nods, then urged his beast forward. They wheeled around mid-air, then dived towards the ball on ground so steeply I felt sure they were going to crash. I watched them with my breath in my throat as I kept Stormclaw gliding through the air. At the last second, Josh said something to his gryff, and they thudded to the ground. The beast immediately sunk his haunches and Josh gripped the saddle horn with one hand, leaning right out of the saddle as he punched a hand through the air and grabbed the ball. Already, his gryff was leaping upwards, stretching his wide wings and pumping them. The motion threw Josh back into the saddle, and he was securely seated again within two wing-beats.

I remembered to breathe again: I'd seen the manoeuvre half a dozen times but it was never any less gut-wrenching. Then I realised he was riding straight at me. I straightened Stormclaw up to ride parallel to Josh, just in time to see him launching the ball through the air to me. I let go of my reins, steering my animal with body weight alone, and snatched the ball out of the air, ignoring the slight sting as the metal handles thumped into my gloved hands. I cast around the rest of the paddock, noting the positions of the rest of the team with a glance. Caleb, matching my pace on my right, was the obvious choice, but I caught a flash of movement racing up on my left and a little below me: Logan. I twisted in my saddle and tossed the ball to him as he drew level. He caught it with ease, rode on a few more wing beats, then threw it cleanly through the hoop. He circled around and landed, and we landed beside him.

"Excellent trius, Josh," he said. "Watch your position on the relaunch – you're a little to the right which is affecting Riverquil's balance. Lyssa, one of your better takes, and nice work spotting me riding in your blindspot. But I shouldn't have been able to catch you at all – Stormclaw is faster than Dartalon. You're holding him back. You've got to trust him."

Easy for him to say – he wasn't the one who'd made a dozen trips to the hospital wing with broken bones after unplanned landings. Still, I nodded in reply. He was right. If we weren't going to let the team down, nothing less than our absolute best would do, and that meant letting go of my fears and pushing the big black and gold beast to fly as fast as he could.

"Again," Logan said. "Liu, toinn manoeuvre. Seb, I want you to block the goal this time."

We all moved our gryffs forward again, but we'd barely taken to the air when a voice sounded from the ground. I glanced down past Stormclaw's shoulder. It was Alden.

"Everyone land," she shouted, waving her arms. "All of you, on the ground!"

Frowning, I took Stormclaw down, and the rest of the team landed around me, with a scraping of talons and a clatter of hooves.

"Practice is cancelled today," she said brusquely.

"But Professor," Logan protested, vaulting from his saddle, "it's the game in two days. This is our last practice."

"It cannot be helped. Everyone dismount and take your gryffs into the stables, then get to the main hall. Quickly, now."

We shared confused glances, and I was first to break the silence.

"Professor, shouldn't we at least turn them out into the fields?"

"Expediency is of the utmost importance. No more discussion, the headmaster expects you all inside the hall in ten minutes. I will escort you."

An uneasiness that had nothing to do with the upcoming game tingled in my stomach, but I swung myself down from Stormclaw's saddle and took hold of his reins. Ten minutes would be a stretch even if we left right now, and I'd pushed my luck enough for one year. Questions would have to wait. The rest of the team evidently felt the same way, as they all dismounted and prepared to lead their gryffs – which was when I spotted Keira's gryff, still tied. Weird.

"I'll get Redwing," the professor said. "Into the barn now, off you go."

We stabled our gryffs, and true to her word, Alden stayed with us right up until we entered the hall. About a quarter of the students had stayed over Christmas, and as near as I could tell, they were all here. I spotted Sam sitting at the fire table and hurried over to join him, along with the rest of our team.

"What's going on?" I asked him. He shrugged.

"No idea. There was an announcement, telling all students and staff to come here immediately."

"Thank you everyone, please settle down," Professor Talendale said, standing up at the head of the professors' table, and raising his hand for quiet. A hush fell over the entire room, every head twisted in his direction. He lowered his hands, and a dark look settled over his eyes. I shot a sidelong look at Sam, but he looked just as puzzled as me.

"I'm afraid I have some bad news," the professor started, after a long pause. "There was an... incident earlier today, involving one of your fellow students."

Dozens of heads whipped round, trying to work out who was missing. I could only think of one person... someone who missed practice today for the first time all year.

"Many of you know Keira Bennett from Fire element," the professor said, his tone grave, and my heart thudded painfully inside my ribcage. "As of an hour ago, she is in the hospital wing, under the close care of Madam Leechington. She was found on the grounds with some... disturbing injuries. I cannot discuss the nature of those injuries with you right now, however we hope that she will make a full recovery, in time."

I swallowed. *Hope? In time?*

"In the meantime, we must all take sensible precautions. Until further notice, student access to the grounds is prohibited, and all outdoor activities will be cancelled."

"But Professor," a voice from our own table called out. Logan. "What about the Itealta match? We need to practice."

"Itealta is cancelled. That is all. You are dismissed. Please return to your common rooms."

For a moment, no-one moved. Logan looked stunned to stone by the news, and his face had taken on a greyish hue.

"But…" he muttered in a stunned voice. "They can't cancel Itealta. They can't…"

"Come on, Logan," Josh said, wrapping an arm around his shoulders while his mouth carried on working soundlessly. "Let's go."

We trudged back to our common room en masse, and we were all back inside by the time the news really sunk in. The team had taken up a couple of the sofas with me and Sam, while the rest of the Fires milled around aimlessly.

"What… what do you think happened to Keira?" I asked.

Logan shook his head.

"I should have known when she didn't show up for practice. I should have known!"

"But what's it got to do with Itealta?" Josh said. "I don't understand why they've cancelled the match."

"Do you think she'll be okay?"

The question silenced all of us. Logan ran a hand over his face, looking ten years older. After a long moment, he pushed himself up from the sofa.

"I'm going to visit her."

"But Logan," Lui said, "Professor Talendale told us all to come here."

"And we came," Logan said. "Now I'm leaving again. The rest of you can stay."

"I'm coming," I said, and before Logan could object, I added, "Safety in numbers, right?"

"Me, too," said Sam, his face a mix of determination and concern.

Logan nodded.

"Okay. The rest of you stay here," he raised a hand as the rest of the team made to get up. "Old Leech will never let the lot of us in."

They sank reluctantly back into their seats, and before we could think better of it, the three of us stepped out of the common room and into the deserted corridor.

We walked in silence, and made it to the hospital wing without meeting a single soul, which was eerie, like the night of Halloween – except this time there was no strange smell, and I managed not to get lost, mainly thanks to Logan and Sam, but in no small part due to the dozen or so visits I'd made this way in the last couple of months. What we hadn't reckoned on was Leechington's reaction to our arrival. She practically turned purple with fury when she saw us and blocked our way before we even set foot in the ward.

"Out! All of you, out, now! Out! No students in the hospital wing."

"Please, Madam Leechington," Logan said, "We just want to see–"

"Absolutely not!" Leechington cut him off, looking horrified at the suggestion. I peered past her and could just about make out a shrunken figure lying in the middle of a bed, but I couldn't make out any more than that – half of her was obscured by the doctor's desk. I frowned, looking at the stack of notes piled on it, and leaned in to Sam.

"Keep her busy," I muttered.

"If we can't see her," Sam said, shifting slightly to one side so she had to turn to look at him, "can you at least tell us what's wrong with her? Please, we're just worried."

Her wrinkled face clouded over with sympathy, and I thought her voice was just a little less harsh when she said,

"I'm sorry. If Professor Talendale had wanted you to know…"

I didn't listen to anymore. Leechington's back was turned to me, and I very carefully took a step towards the door to the ward, watching her closely. Logan's eyes widened as he saw me, and then he started peppering the healer with questions like a pro, keeping her attention and making enough noise that she couldn't hear my footsteps as I slipped inside.

I didn't waste any time, hurrying over to her desk and looking down at the notes. Keira's name was written across the top, and under it was a diagram of her body, with several patches of bruising drawn onto it, and what looked like… I couldn't be sure, but, well, it looked like it might have been a set of toothmarks on her shoulder.

I supressed a shudder and scanned the rest of the document. According to the neat handwriting, Keira was found out on the grounds just before practice started, near the Lost Meadow. I knew the spot: I'd passed in on my way to the Unhallowed Grove on Halloween. I read on. She was unconscious when one of the dragon riders saw her, and she hadn't woken on the way back to the castle, or since, despite the healer's attempts to rouse her. The toothmarks were already showing signs of infection, which the healer had magically stemmed.

It looked like we'd interrupted her halfway through writing the report, but the words 'beatha potion' were written in red ink and underlined twice. I heard Logan's raised voice and looked up – Leechington was looking increasingly irritated by the disruption, I could tell even from here.

"Now really boys, I must get back to my patient…"

Time was up. I hurried back across the ward and slipped out of the door, rejoining the group just as she turned to go back inside. She eyed me suspiciously, then walked past me and back to Keira's bedside.

"Well? Did you find anything?" Sam asked.

"Nothing good. Come on, let's get going. I'll fill you in on the way."

Chapter Eighteen

Two days later, we were no closer to finding out what the beatha potion was, or more importantly, what it was used for. We had plenty of time to spend researching, given that we were confined to the castle, and that meant no work and no Itealta practice, and we still had a couple of days until classes started. The problem was that there was only one place we could get information, and that was the library – and there were thousands of books, any one of which might contain a reference to the obscure potion. There was only so much time we could spend in there before someone noticed we were acting weirdly.

On the plus side, Kelsey had arrived back at the academy and she was the perfect cover story. Unlike me and Sam, she was no stranger to spending hours in the library. If nothing else, our search was likely to be more organised now she was back.

"You take 'Venomous Cryptids' and 'Deadly Aquatic Creatures'," she told me, dumping a pair of massive, dusty books on the table in front of me, and then dumped another pair in front of Sam. "You can look through 'Magical Anti-Vemons' and 'Herbology for Healing'. And I'll check 'Supernatural Contagious Diseases'."

"How come you only have to check one?" Sam said, and Kelsey pulled a huge tome that had to be as thick as it was wide from the shelf, staggering slightly under its weight as she brought it over to our table.

"Oh."

"Is there still no news about Keira?" she asked, wiping dust from the front of the book, and easing its ancient cover open with a creak. I shook my head.

"Nope. At least, none that they're sharing with us."

"It's so weird. What was she even doing out there? I know she liked to walk the grounds, but she never normally went anywhere near the grove. She said it made her nervous, she didn't even like it being that close to the academy."

She wasn't the only one who held that opinion, not now that I knew what was out there.

"Never?" Sam said, turning the page in his book.

"She preferred to walk by the lake."

I snorted.

"Like that's so much safer."

Kelsey shrugged.

"She's just lucky there was a dragon rider flying that way." She paused, mid-way through scanning a page. "Have you spoken to the rider yet?"

I shook my head, looking up from my book for a moment – my vision was starting to blur from staring at the tiny faded words inked into the paper.

"We don't know which one it was."

"Well, it shouldn't be hard to find out. There are only two of them."

"There are?"

Kelsey sighed in exasperation.

"Am I the only one who pays attention to anything the professors say?"

Me and Sam shared a look, and both nodded.

"Yup, pretty much."

"Honestly! Dragon riders are incredibly rare, only a couple in every generation. Dragons won't let just anyone climb on their backs, you know. You have to be chosen. There are three dragons here at the academy, but only two have riders. I heard the rider of the third dragon died, or went missing, no-one's exactly sure, about twenty years ago. Dardyr has been surly ever since, he won't even let anyone anywhere near him, let alone touch or ride him. It's like he's mourning his rider. It's really sad."

"Yeah, heart-breaking," I said, picturing the bad-tempered beast I'd occasionally seen blasting fire at students who ventured too close to the dragons' enclosure.

"Anyway, that means it has to have been either Paethio or Zoynenth's rider who saw you – Ethan or Talia." She paused, thinking. "Ethan is a water element, so we should probably talk to Talia instead."

"Keira's in hospital, really sick. I think this is a little more important than elemental animosity. Besides, aren't dragon riders supposed to be above all that – you know, attuned to all the elements through their dragons?"

Kelsey narrowed her eyes at me.

"You *have* been paying attention to Alden."

"Sometimes. I try not to make a habit of it, it gives her unrealistic expectations of me."

"Well, as it happens, you're right – in theory, at least. But something about Ethan makes me uneasy, so let's try Talia first anyway, yeah?"

I buried a chuckle and nodded as I turned back to my book.

"Sure. I doubt whoever saw will be able to tell us much, anyway."

"I say we go and ask her now," Sam said, looking up from his book hopefully. Kelsey quickly dashed his hopes.

"The potion is more important, if we can work out what it does then we'll know what's wrong with Keira. Besides, we shouldn't all go looking for Talia, it will look weird. One of us should keep researching."

"Oh, no," Sam said. "If you think I'm spending more time in this library than absolutely necessary..."

I coughed and arched a brow at him.

"What I meant was," he amended quickly, "is that you're so much better at this research stuff than I am. We can't spare you."

"Fine," Kelsey sighed. "I'll stay and keep looking. But finish up those books you're going through first, okay? I still think this is our best lead."

We got through the books in record time, but it was still over an hour later when we stumbled out of the library, bleary-eyed and fuzzy-brained.

I stretched my arms out over my head, wincing at the audible click from my shoulders – one too many Itealta injuries, probably – and started down the corridor.

"Where shall we check first?" I asked Sam. He checked his watch.

"Well, it's dinner time, so it's probably worth checking the main hall first, right?"

"And let me guess, get some food while we're there?"

"It's important not to look out of place," he said, with a touch of smugness. "Besides, we can grab something for Kelsey, too, so she doesn't miss dinner."

A few minutes later, we both had food-laden plates, and I had a box Aiden the kitchen mage had kindly filled with a couple of steaks and half a tray of mash for Kelsey.

If there's one thing I learned last semester, it's that you don't keep a werewolf from her food. We took our seats on the Fire table, keeping a watchful eye on the green table that belonged to the Earth elements.

"There," I said, when we were half-way through our food, nodding to a tall red-head who was taking a seat at the end of the Earth table. "That's her."

We ate the rest of our food, oblivious to the conversation going on down the rest of our table around us, keeping one eye on the dragon rider. I was wondering whether we should wait until she was finished when Sam stacked our plates and walked over to her. I hurried to catch up with him.

"Hi, it's Talia, isn't it?" he said. "I'm Sam, this is Lyssa."

The rider looked up at us, her face impossible to read. After a moment, she looked at me and said,

"You're one of the reserves on Fire's Itealta team, aren't you? Tough break about the match being cancelled. We were looking forward to you beating Air."

"Actually, that's kinda what we wanted to talk to you about," I said.

"I can't help." She broke eye contact with me and I got the sense people had already asked her. "I don't have any influence."

"No, I don't mean that," I said quickly. "It's about Keira. Were you… were you the one who found her?"

Her expression turned sympathetic and she set her cutlery down.

"I can't help with that, either, but I was sorry to hear about it. It was Ethan who found her." She chewed her lip a moment, and then seemed to reach a decision. "A word of advice? If you're going to speak to him, go alone, just you. He has an eye for a pretty face."

I gave her a grateful smile, even as my insides churned. I was hardly classic honeytrap material.

"Thanks."

"I wish I could do more. I hope Keira recovers soon."

"Yeah, me too."

It was, of course, too much to hope we'd be that lucky twice – there was no sign of Ethan at his elemental table. He'd obviously eaten and left.

"You might as well head back to the library," I told Sam as we headed out of the hall. "Kelsey's probably starving."

"Alright," Sam said, sounding reluctant – though whether it was returning to the library, or missing out on speaking to the dragon rider that he was unhappy about, I wasn't sure. "Just… just be careful, okay? This guy sounds like a real jerk."

Ah. I guess that answered my question. I shot him the most confident smile I could muster.

"I'll be fine. He's nothing I can't handle."

I watched Sam until he disappeared from sight, then ran a quick hand through my hair, making sure it wasn't a total mess, and headed towards the Water common room. I'd never been there, so it was a little tricky, but eventually I managed to track it down. Of course, I couldn't get in without the password, so I was forced to loiter outside like a total stalker. I didn't even know for sure that he was inside, even if I did manage to convince one of the Waters to let me in, which seemed unlikely. As plans went, it was pretty terrible, but it was the best I had. With a sigh, I leaned back against the wall and resigned myself to a long wait.

"You forget the password? Wait, you're not one of our first years."

I jerked my head to the left and saw the tall, dark-haired guy regarding me with suspicion. Too bad I had other priorities, because he was kinda cute, in a rugged, brooding sort of way.

"I'm looking for Ethan Salford," I said, cursing my cheeks that I could already feel burning. Cute guy's mouth curved into a smile.

"Then you're in luck." He held out a hand. "I'm Ethan."

I made to shake his hand, but he caught my fingers in his, and raised my hand to his lips. I just about managed to keep from rolling my eyes as he kissed it, watching me through mischievous eyes. After a moment it became clear he had no intention of letting go.

"Uh, can I have my hand back?"

He smiled again and released it.

"This is normally the part where you'd tell me your name."

As if any part of this was normal. This guy was way too full of himself, probably used to getting anything he wanted through his good looks and dragon rider status. Despite that, the annoying flush stayed in my cheeks and my heart was beating just a little harder than usual. I'd be flattered by his attention if I didn't suspect he fancied himself more than he fancied me.

"I'm Lyssa, Lyssa Eldridge," I told him, forcing a smile onto my lips. His eyes sharpened with interest.

"The Itealta player everyone's talking about."

"I mean, I don't think everyone's talking about me," I said, tucking a stray strand of hair behind my ear. "I'm just a reserve."

"Modest, too," he said, flashing me another of those breath-taking smiles. "The most raw potential anyone has seen in years is what they say. Too bad you're a Fire… or are you?"

He cocked his head just slightly. Clearly, my Itealta potential wasn't the only thing people had been talking about. That was the trouble with places like Dragondale: it was practically impossible to keep anything quiet, not least when someone did the allegedly impossible and manifested two opposing elements. I didn't want to admit that I still had almost no control over my water power, so I just shrugged and gave what I hoped was a self-depreciating smile.

"Well, I am honoured that you sought me out, Lyssa Eldridge." He gave a short, mocking bow, his eyes sparkling with amusement. "What can I do for you?"

"I heard it was you who found Keira."

"The Fire girl. Most unfortunate," he said, not sounding particularly sincere.

"It was you, then?" I pressed, and decided a little flattery couldn't hurt my cause. "I heard you saved her life."

He obviously liked the sound of that, standing straighter and squaring his hips to me. Eugh. I forced a smile to play across my lips.

"I was hoping you'd tell me about it."

"I'd be happy to – but I need to ensure Paethio has been properly fed. I was just heading there now. You're welcome to join me."

"Funny, it looked like you were heading to the common room."

I jerked my head at the door we were standing beside, and he just grinned.

"Appearances can be deceptive." He turned on his heel and started back along the corridor, then looked at me over his shoulder, one eyebrow raised in what was unmistakably a challenge. "Coming?"

Like I had a choice. I followed him through the corridors and out of the main door into the grounds, hoping that no-one was watching us, because he might have special dispensation to leave the castle, but I sure as hell didn't. And much as I wanted to find out about Keira, I didn't want to get myself expelled doing it. Or, like, eaten by a dragon.

It was dark outside, and a layer of frost was already forming on the short grass.

"This way," Ethan said, beckoning me towards a stone building looming in the distance. I heard a loud snort as I passed the gryff barn, and with a pang of longing I recognised the sound of Stormclaw's squeal.

"Sorry boy," I muttered under my breath. If I went inside to see him, the rest of the animals would kick up such a fuss that we were bound to be caught. I hurried to keep up with Ethan and he reached the stone building just in front of me, and held open the door.

"Have you ever seen a dragon up close?" he asked, as I stepped inside. I shook my head, staring around me in amazement – it was much bigger in here than it had appeared from outside. Like Ares' enclosure, it was as if I'd stepped through the wardrobe into Narnia, only this place was much, much bigger than the gryphon's home.

"It's enchanted," Ethan said, as I twisted round, looking up at the ceilings that were so far above me I could barely make them out. "Apparently it would have ruined the view."

He shrugged with apparent carelessness, but he was watching me closely. My eyes drifted back down from the high ceilings and the immaculate stone walls to the cobbled floor. The hall we were in wasn't just tall, it covered a huge amount of ground, and a few hundred paces away was the building's fourth wall, which stood only a couple of feet high, so that you could comfortably lean on it and look out. Beyond was a wide expanse of dusty, scorched earth. I walked over, no longer in control of my own limbs, staring out into the landscape that was most definitely not visible from anywhere else on the academy grounds. And I knew – I'd flown over all of them. Rocks jutted up from the earth, and only a few tall trees stood stoutly against the rugged terrain.

"It covers over two hundred acres," Ethan said, and I got the feeling he was enjoying me being dumbstruck. I made an effort to compose myself and squinted up at the sky. Could I just about make out three dark shadows in the distance? Ethan laughed, and let out a long, low whistle.

There was a distant screech, and one of the shapes circled away from the others. I watched, awestruck, as the massive creature glided effortlessly through the night sky, its wings spread wide on either side of its long, scaled body. It drew closer, and I could see how different its wings were from Stormclaw's. Where the gryff's wings were birdlike, thick, arc-shaped, and covered in feathers, the dragon's wings were far more angular and I could make out the bone structure which seemed only to have a paper-thin layer of skin smeared over them. As it drew closer still, I realised everything about it was bigger than I'd first thought. No wonder they needed such a vast enclosure. The force of the wind displaced by his massive wings blew my hair out of my face, and the dragon screeched again. I winced in pain, near deafened by the dragon's cry, as his feet crunched down onto the ground with a thud I could feel through my feet. His reptilian face was completely covered in scales other than his eyes, which were watching me with unsettling intelligence as he tucked his wings back to his sides, and stretched his head over the low wall, bumping his nose to Ethan's hand.

"Magnificent, isn't he?"

"Very," I breathed, and then shook myself out of my trance. It was true, Paethio was an incredible animal, and I couldn't believe I was standing this close to him – to a freaking *dragon*, for crying out loud. But I was here for a reason, and that reason wasn't to inflate Ethan's ego – he clearly didn't need any help in that department.

"So, you were telling me about Keira," I prompted.

"Oh, she's not interested in us," Ethan said mournfully to his dragon, rubbing his hand across the creature's wide nostrils. "Some girls are just impossible to impress."

"I am impressed," I promised him. "Paethio is amazing. I just really need to know what happened with Keira."

Ethan dropped his hand and turned back to me.

"We were doing a perimeter lap – you know that us riders are responsible for making sure that no-one crosses the forcefield protecting the academy, right? – and I decided to do a flyover by the Unhallowed Grove. There are some real nasty things lurking in that place, and I like to make sure they stay put. Make sure everyone can sleep soundly in their beds. Anyway, I saw something lying on the ground and came down for a closer look, and found Keira lying there, unconscious."

"What was wrong with her?"

"Who knows? She wasn't bleeding, she wasn't injured, it was just like she'd fallen asleep. Except I couldn't wake her."

"She wasn't bleeding?" The report had definitely shown bite marks on her shoulder, and if she'd been bitten, there should have been blood. "Are you sure?"

Ethan's brow furrowed and he looked annoyed. He obviously wasn't used to being questioned. I backtracked quickly.

"I just meant, it was dark and that. It would have been easy to miss... not that I'm saying you'd miss something."

He seemed to come to a decision, and smiled, relaxing.

"I wasn't mistaken. There was no blood. Even if I hadn't seen it, Paethio would have smelled it. No blood, no obvious injuries."

"Did you get a look at what attacked her? Or see anything weird?"

"Attacked her? Nope, she was alone. Nothing strange other than the unconscious girl. Oh, except... there was this smell, I couldn't quite place it, but," he paused, frowning, then continued, "I don't know. It was disgusting, like maybe something was rotting? It really set Paethio on edge, that's for sure. Anyway, enough talk about Keira."

He reached out to me and brushed a lock of hair out of my face, then bent his lips to mine. I planted my hand firmly on his chest.

"Whoa. What are you doing?"

"What does it look like?" he asked with a smile, leaning in again, and again I pushed him back. He glared at me, curling his lip.

"Seriously? *You're* rejecting *me*? You're not going to find anyone better here."

"I'm going back to the castle now," I told him, forcing my voice to remain calm and firm, and ignoring the pounding inside my ribcage. "I'll see you around."

Chapter Nineteen

L yssa! Where have you been?"

I almost jumped right out of my skin when the voice sounded from behind me, right as I was slipping back into the entrance hall. Heart pounding, I turned round and found myself face to face with Sam.

"Don't do that! I was with Ethan. What's wrong?"

I added that last as I took in his pale, anxious face, and the restless way his eyes were darting around.

"It's Kelsey, she's gone."

"Gone?"

"She wasn't in the library when I got back there. Dawson said she left with Underwood, and she didn't look happy."

I frowned. It was a full moon tonight, but it was still early, she had a couple of hours before she needed to take off for the grove. The grove that had some strange new danger in it, if Ethan was telling the truth about Keira. Professor Underwood must have been taking her somewhere else, there was no other reason he would come and get her. Whatever was out there, it must have the professors really riled if they didn't think a werewolf could handle it.

"Where did he take her?"

"I don't know. Dean said he saw them heading down to the dungeons. I'm going there now."

I blanched. They were going to lock her in a cage. She'd made so much progress controlling her full moon shifted form, but if she was trapped in a dark room with nothing to distract her from her bestial nature, there was no telling how much damage it would do to her and how far it would set her back. And I didn't just mean in terms of her shift.

"I'm coming too. Which way?"

We hurried through the deserted corridors, keeping our heads down and our thoughts to ourselves, but I didn't doubt we were both thinking the same thing. We needed to get to her before she hurt herself.

"And just where are you two going?"

The voice sounded from behind us, and we spun around.

"Professor…" Sam stammered.

"The pair of you should be in your dormitories. The semester starts tomorrow."

"Yes, Professor Atherton," I said. "We're heading there now."

He narrowed his eyes.

"Where have you been?"

"We were in the library," I said, which wasn't a complete lie. We *had* been in the library. We'd just been other places since.

"Lyssa was worried about being behind when classes start," Sam added, and I only didn't kick him because Atherton was watching us closely.

"I'm glad to see you're finally taking your studies seriously, Ms Eldridge," the professor said, staring at me through hooded eyes. "I'll see you in class tomorrow. See that you don't loiter on your way back to your room."

He turned in a whirl of robes, and walked back along the corridor, following the trail of blazing fireballs. I watched him until he was out of sight.

"Come on, let's go."

We increased our pace, hurrying down the hallway, until the fireballs hanging near the ceiling became less vibrant, marking our entrance to the less-visited parts of the castle.

"What did you find out from Ethan?"

"Aside from the fact he loves himself?" I shook my head. "Not much. He was just using it as an excuse to make a move on me. He did mention that there was no blood, though."

"That's weird," Sam said, as we rounded another corner. "I thought bites were supposed to bleed? The body's way of getting rid of infection, or something, right?"

"Yeah, I thought so, too. But she definitely wasn't bleeding."

We mulled that over in silence as we walked. We'd almost made it to the dungeon when Sam stopped walking and touched a hand to my arm.

"What's that?"

"What's—"

I cut off as I heard a scraping somewhere in the shadows behind us. Straining my ears, I could just about make out the scratching of claws on stone. I spun around and backed away, searching the darkness for whatever awful creature was creeping around down here. Slowly, with bestial grace, it slipped from the shadows.

"Toby!"

I let out a breath and a nervous chuckle slipped out with it.

"I swear that animal is trying to give me a heart attack. Go on, get out of here."

I shooed him away but he just looked at me through his wide brown eyes, and if I didn't know better, I'd say he looked amused. Whatever. He was the least of my concerns right now. We carried on, and he followed us the rest of the way to the dungeon entrance. The door was shut and I glanced at Sam for a moment, then grabbed the handle and eased it open.

It took my eyes a moment to adjust to the gloom as we stepped inside, and shut the door behind us, leaving Toby in the corridor.

"What are you doing here?" a voice — not Kelsey's — snapped, and as we turned around, the dull lights flickering over our faces, we saw Professor Underwood's eyes sharpen with recognition. "Ah, I should have known. Nothing stays quiet for long around here, does it?"

I didn't reply, because my eyes were darting around the room I'd first glimpsed on Halloween, only tonight it was completely transformed. There was no music, no buffet table, and no students — except one. Kelsey was in a cell at the back of the room, with heavy chains bolting her to the wall.

"It's probably for the best," the professor said, kindly. "Kelsey will need all the support we can give her this evening."

"What's..." My voice caught in my throat a moment as I watched my friend who was sitting on the stone floor, showing not a flicker of recognition at the sound of our voices. "What's wrong with her?"

"She's in a trance. I hope that by preparing herself fully before the transformation comes over her, she will better be able to control herself when it happens."

"You seem to know a lot about it."

"Alas, not enough, I fear. Co-operation between magical academies has its limits, particularly when it comes to sharing pack secrets for the education of one whose very existence is frowned upon."

The professor rose from his seat and pulled up two more chairs.

"It's going to be a long night. She won't be able to hear you in her trance, but I don't doubt you will be of great comfort to her once the transformation begins."

*

Professor Underwood was right: it was a long night. I thought I'd seen dark things, felt every type of pain, but when Kelsey's transformation began, I started to realise exactly how sheltered I'd been. Never in my life had I seen anything so horrific, nor been so helpless to do anything, as when the moon's spell fell over my friend and wracked her body with agony so absolute that I couldn't tell the difference between her human and lupine howls of agony. And that was only the beginning, as she clawed and bit at her chains and her own limbs, desperate to escape and answer the call of the moon. At times it seemed like dawn would never come, but eventually it did, and when Kelsey's human form returned, the three of us helped her back to her dorm, and got what rest we could before the rising sun summoned us to classes.

Under orders from Talendale himself, we gathered in the entrance hall and waited to be escorted to our Botany class out in the academy's vast greenhouses. At least we were partnered with the Earth elements in this class, which meant I wouldn't have to put up with Felicity's sneering gibes until Atherton's class. It was just as well, given how awful I felt this morning.

I stifled a yawn as we entered the humid greenhouses, trying my best not to let Kelsey see how tired I was – she felt bad enough about last night, no matter how many times we told her we were glad we were able to be there with her. I just hoped whatever was lurking in the Unhallowed Grove, it was caught before the next full moon.

"Good morning, everyone, good morning," Professor Ellerby said, clapping her hands to get everyone's attention. "Today we shall be working on a particularly important task. You will all, of course, be aware that poor Keira remains in the hospital wing."

Immediately, the entire class fell so silent you could practically hear the plants around us growing. Everyone wanted to know what had happened to Keira, but none of the professors had so far said a word about it.

"We will be repotting and assisting the growth of the Beathanian plant, which will be essential in treating Keira's injuries. I expect you to work with the utmost care

218

and attention. Each of you will partner with a student from a different element. Quickly, now."

The class broke itself up, and I found myself partnered with a serious Earth element called Ben Ackerman. I'd seen him in our other classes last semester, of course, but I hadn't worked with him before.

"Collect one plant and one large pot from my desk please, and take them back to your tables. I will inspect each plant before the end of the lesson, and I expect to see at least half an inch of growth."

I raised my eyebrows but said nothing. Half an inch was a lot, given that this lesson was only an hour long. Ben, at least, didn't appear to be worried.

"You get the pot and some soil," he said. "I'll choose us a plant."

And that was where working with an earth element really came in helpful in Botany. Their powers might *seem* less impressive at first glance, but when it came to being in tune with nature, there was no-one better. All druids had a certain affinity for nature, be it flora or fauna, but none so much as the Earths. I grabbed a pot and some potting soil, content in the knowledge that Ben would bring us a decent plant which would have every chance of making the half-inch growth.

He set the plant onto our muddied wooden desk, running his fingers over the stem lightly.

"Couldn't you have found one that looked a little healthier?" I asked, tossing a few handfuls of soil into the new pot. Ben's lips moved a fraction in response, in what I took to be a smile.

"Trust me, we got the best one."

I squinted at the drooping, sickly-looking plant, then glanced round the rest of the tables at the array of bushy, perky Beathanians. I did, however, notice more than one earth element looking enviously at our half-dead plant.

"You're the plant guy. Want me to soak this soil?"

"Just a sprinkle. A little bit more… yeah, there."

I set the watering can aside and helped him ease the plant from its old pot, taking care not to disturb the roots, but to my surprise, Ben dusted the soil from them.

"Little bit of heat," he said, "Just here, on the roots."

I shrugged, then lifted my right hand, holding it above the roots and letting a small amount of heat leak out of it – about the equivalent of holding your hand above a lightbulb that's been on for a couple of hours. I might have imagined it, or maybe Ben's hand shook, but the plant seemed to give a little shiver as the warmth reached it. After about a minute, Ben nodded and I dropped my hand, not at all surprised to see the plant looking just a little healthier. We settled it into the pot, and I spent the next half hour alternately applying heat and drops of water, while Ben stroked the plant's stem and leaves, and occasionally touched his fingers to the soil.

"Very good," Ellerby said when she reached our table. "This is plant number fourteen, correct?"

She glanced down at the sheet on her clipboard held in her mud-stained hands.

"Let's get it measured, then."

She held a stick to the moist soil, and measured to the very tip of the plant, then jotted the number down on her clipboard and beamed at us.

"Excellent work. Over an inch of growth. Everyone else could stand to learn a lesson from you. Get yourselves cleaned up and I'll escort you all back to the castle."

Unfortunately, the rest of our classes didn't go as smoothly as Botany. After breakfast we had Spellcraft and Professor Atherton spent the entire time glowering at me, no doubt wondering why I couldn't answer a single question, despite having allegedly spent all of yesterday evening ensconced in the library, studying.

Felicity, of course, answered every question I couldn't, earning her looks of approval from Atherton and glares from all the Fires in the room – except for the ones who were glaring at me. Professor Atherton had decided to assign all of our element group extra homework to make up for my deficiencies. Just as well my work at the gryff barn was still on hold, because I'd never have had time to get this lot done on top of everything else.

The trend continued throughout the week – every professor piled more and more work on us, telling us we had to start getting prepared for our end of year exams. Not that we had any time to revise with all the extra work they were setting. I was so wrapped up with my workload that it wasn't until Friday evening at dinner that I started to pay attention to the murmurs of some of the other students.

"I heard Janey Dobson from Earth element found him," Sharna said, her voice a conspiratorial whisper as she looked round the table to make sure everyone was listening. Dean nodded enthusiastically.

"It's true. No-one knows how long he'd been down there, but no-one saw him at breakfast that morning. No-one even knows if he went to bed the night before."

"You mean he might have been lying there all night and all day?" Liu said.

"Imagine if Janey hadn't taken that shortcut," Sharna said, gleefully. "He could have been there for days before anyone found him. He might even have died."

Liu shuddered. I set my fork down and looked across the table at them.

"Who?"

"Where've you been, Lyssa?" Sharna said, looking stunned that I wasn't up to date with the latest gossip. "Ethan, of course. He was found in the lower corridors, on a shortcut between Earth and Water dorms. Someone attacked him."

"Or some*thing*," Dean put in, taking a spoonful of some brown sludge on his plate that I didn't care to identify.

"Do you think it's the same thing that attacked Keira?" Sam said. I stamped on his foot before he could let on that we knew more about that than we should. "Or the same person," he amended hastily.

"It's a bit too much of a coincidence if it's not, don't you think?" Sharna said. "Two attacks only a couple of weeks apart."

"But Keira was found outside in the grounds," Kelsey pointed out. "You can't think whatever did that to her has found a way inside the castle, it would never have got past the academy's defences, and the professors would never allow something dangerous to roam the hallways. I mean, they just wouldn't, would they?"

I placed my hand lightly over hers, and she took a breath for the first time in a minute, looking frantic.

"How else could it have happened?" Sharna said with a careless shrug, completely oblivious to the fact Kelsey was on the verge of panic – which was nothing out of the ordinary for Sharna. When she got her teeth into the latest piece of gossip, she tended not to notice anything else. Which was convenient, because otherwise she'd have seen the blood drain from my face. A second attack. I'd only spoken to him a handful of days before. Sure, he was a jerk, and he was a bit full of himself, but he didn't deserve to be attacked. And worse, he'd been our only witness, or the closest thing we'd had to one. I'd still been hoping he would remember some detail that would give us a clue. Could that have been why he was attacked?

"We should get going," I said, quickly stacking my plate on top of Kelsey and Sam's, who looked startled for a moment but recovered quickly. "We need to make a start on our homework."

Chapter Twenty

H i, mum, it's me. Lyssa," I said into the phone pressed against my ear.

"Lyssa, how wonderful to hear from you!" Her voice sounded genuine, if a little shocked. This was the first time I'd phoned since that first time I'd been sitting in Professor Talendale's office, telling her that I'd come here to study. I looked idly around Talendale's office now, noting that nothing in here had really changed over the last six months – except me. I'd never been anxious about speaking to my own mum before. And I'd sworn that I wouldn't have this conversation over the phone, but there were three people in the hospital wing now, and none of them showed any sign of making a recovery any time soon. Academy security had been stepped up, but that hadn't stopped Professor Ellerby getting attacked just three weeks after Ethan. And if a professor could be attacked, how could any of us be sure we were safe? The answer was that we couldn't, and that was why I had to make this call. If something happened to me... Well, I just had to know the truth. It was important. Almost as important as hearing my mum's voice again. Letters just weren't the same.

"Sorry it's been so long, mum." I glanced across the room at Professor Talendale, who was pretending to be occupied sorting his living bookcases, in an unusual display of tact. His efforts weren't being helped by the shelves occasionally reordering themselves and jumbling up his attempts, which didn't deter him from trying.

"Lyssa? Did you hear me?"

"Sorry," I said, shaking my head and focussing back on my call.

"Never mind, it's not important. What's wrong? You don't sound like your usual self."

I stared down at the desk in front of me, the same desk that had revealed the truth about my heritage, and wondered how this was supposed to go. I'd been right: it wasn't a phone call sort of conversation. I couldn't quite seem to find the words.

"I…" I sighed. I couldn't do it to her. Adopted or not, she deserved the right to tell me on her own terms. "I miss you."

I heard her own sigh travel down the line. When she spoke again, she sounded years older, and took her time over each word.

"Lyssa, that's not why you called, and we both know it. You've always been able to talk to me. Tell me what's bothering you."

I hesitated. I didn't want to bring this up on the phone, but I didn't want to lie in what might be our last ever conversation, either, and it seemed like I was going to have to choose one. In the end, I went with the one that seemed less disrespectful to the woman who taught me right from wrong.

"Am I adopted?" I blurted the words with less tact than I intended, and listened to her sharp intake of breath and the silence that followed with guilt clawing at my throat.

"I– *We* should have talked to you before you left. We meant to, you know, before you went to university, but it all happened so suddenly."

It felt like my insides were made of lead. I'd expected her to laugh and ask me where I got such a ridiculous idea from, but I'd been wrong. Very wrong. I was adopted.

"I want you to know this doesn't change anything, Lyssa. No matter where you came from, I *am* your mother, and your dad is still your dad, and we love you, very much."

"And Holly? Is she–?"

"The doctors said we would never conceive. When I got pregnant a couple of years after you came to us, it was completely unexpected. But we love you both the same. You're *both* our daughters."

At least now I knew why Holly was so much better than me academically, why she'd been so much more like our dad. Her dad.

"Lyssa? Are you still there?"

"Yeah," I said, dully.

"We came to this country for you, Lyssa."

That sharpened my attention. They'd always changed the subject when I brought up the reason they moved to England, brushing it off as wanting a change of scenery, or there being better work opportunities than in America.

"When your birth mother gave you up, it was with two stipulations – that you kept your name, and that you were raised in England. We agreed without hesitation, and we would not change that for anything. Not for anything. You're part of this family, and blood doesn't have anything to do with it. I love you, Lyssa, and nothing will ever change that."

"I love you, too, mum," I said, numbly forcing my mouth to make the words. "I've got to go. I'll see you soon."

I hung the phone up and sat for the longest moment, staring blankly at the living wood desk the phone was sitting on. My birth mother had wanted me to stay in England. So I could come to this academy? Be raised a druid? I snorted softly to myself. That had worked out well. And just as I thought I was starting to find my place in the world, find somewhere I belonged, it turned out I didn't even belong in my own family. Not either of them.

I heard someone clear their throat and looked up to see Professor Talendale had abandoned his bookshelf and was watching me. Instead of ushering me from his office and back to my lessons, he eased himself into his chair.

"It's never easy to learn we're not who we thought we were," he said. "But when it comes to it, we find that it's not who we are that matters, so much as those we choose to surround ourselves with. It is a noble thing to raise a child who is not your own." He steepled his hands and stared at me over the top of them. "And it is a noble thing to choose the company of those others ostracise, those who have nothing to offer you but themselves. Nobility, perhaps then, is a learned behaviour."

I stared back into his dark eyes, surrounded by wrinkles and a few white hairs.

"Family comes in many forms, Lyssa. Do not turn your back on one in search of another."

I kept staring at him, dumbstruck, and he leaned back in his chair and his customary frown returned to his face.

"Now, back to class with you. There are only seven weeks remaining before your exams, and Professor Atherton tells me you can't afford to squander them."

I got up to leave his office, the door opening itself at my approach, before I could say something that would land me in hot water – like that Professor Atherton was so biased it was amazing he even knew the name of any student outside of Air element.

Life at the academy had become strange since the last attack – well, stranger, at least – and one of the new rules was that students were prohibited from roaming the hallways alone. As such, the open doorway took on a shimmering quality, and as I peered into the water-like surface, I caught a glimpse of hundreds of books lining ancient shelves, and a dozen or so students, amongst them Kelsey and Sam. Professor Talendale had conjured me a portal to the library, though whether because he thought I should be studying, or that I ought be with my misfit friends, I wasn't exactly sure. Probably both. I took a breath and stepped through.

We hadn't been in the library for long when Professor Sumner arrived to escort us to Botany class. Though Professor Ellerby was in the hospital wing, our classes had continued uninterrupted, though without her careful instruction there'd been a steady downturn in the class's progress. Most notably, nearly all of the Beathanian plants had wilted, and several had died completely. Mine and Ben's was the only one that was still growing strong, and I'd heard a rumour that it was now being kept under guard day and night, and would be until it was ready to be harvested for the Beatha potion. One plant would be enough, Professor Sumner had quietly assured me, so long as it remained healthy. I barely trusted myself anywhere near it – what if I turned up the heat too much and it caught fire? – but Ben brushed aside my concerns and guided me attentively. We'd been excused from participating in the rest of the Botany lessons, and I'd even once been called out of Spellcraft to tend to it, much to Professor Atherton's annoyance, and my amusement. Of course, he'd punished me by setting double homework so my victory had been short-lived, but a win was still a win.

When I wasn't tending the Beathanian plant, or visiting Stormclaw under close escort – because he'd become so surly in my absence that he'd landed a couple of the assistants in the hospital wing and Madam Leechington had griped that she didn't need to extra work distracting her from her other patients – I was in the library or the common room, cramming for our exams. Even my attempts at the skin-walking spell had been put on hold – although that was probably for the best. I had enough to worry about right now. It didn't help that I had no idea what to expect. Dean had been telling everyone that when his brother was in first year, the Supernatural Zoology exam had involved touching Ares, the academy's notoriously aggressive gryphon, but no-one quite knew whether to believe him.

Kelsey had spent days memorising dates of important Goblin rebellions, and notable cases in the court of magical law, while Sam had taken a more practical approach and was setting fire to anything he could get his hands on, then reducing the temperature of the flame before it could do any serious damage.

As for me, well, I just hoped my natural talent with magical creatures would be enough to make up for my deficiencies in Spellcraft and a whole year of not paying attention in Potions.

Time has a nasty habit of speeding up right when you want it to slow down. The days and weeks passed in the blink of an eye, and before I knew it, the exams were upon us, and I was woefully under-prepared. Not, as I'd told Kelsey bitterly, that I'd have felt prepared if I'd had another six months.

Written exams were first – Gaelic, History of Magic and Druidic Law, and I'd have been hard pressed to decide which one was worse. Suffice to say, I wasn't expecting to have a career in law enforcement by the time my results came back.

For Botany, Professor Sumner took us each into a room with twenty plants that we had to identify, state their uses and their ideal growing conditions. I got six for sure, but the rest were a combination of educated guesses and made up answers.

Things picked up after that, though. Professor Swann set a series of candles, alternating black and white, in a circle and told me to set the wick of the first alight, then cause the flame to leap to each of the black candles without touching any of the white, or causing the wax to melt. Behind her were a small pile of singed white candles, so I knew someone had found it harder than I had.

Supernatural Zoology was a piece of cake – we had to demonstrate safe handling of a gryff, and several smaller animals I'd dealt with a couple of times. No gryphons or dragons, which was just as well, since Paethio had become more and more unpredictable with each day he spent without Ethan.

The Beathanian plant was just days away from being ready to be harvested, and it couldn't happen soon enough. Paethio had already taken to shooting bursts of fire at anyone who looked at him the wrong way. The whole grounds were covered in scorch marks.

We had two exams a day for the whole week, except Friday when we only had one. The one I'd been dreading. Professor Atherton's Spellcraft exam. And it was even worse than I'd feared. I hardly managed any of the incantations, and I could barely conjure even the most basic of glamours. When I stepped out, bleary-eyed, I almost walked straight into Sam.

"Well, that was brutal," he said, stretching his arms out over his head and yawning loudly.

"Only for those of us who aren't gifted in the finer arts," Felicity said tartly from behind him. Sam rolled his eyes.

"We might all have to wait here to be escorted back to our common rooms," Kelsey said, "but that doesn't mean we have to speak to you."

"Touchy," she said, giving us a smile that was all teeth, and turning back to Paisley and Cecelia. "Do you smell that, girls? It's the stench of failure."

"That must be why it's strongest around you," I said sweetly. "Must be terrible, knowing Daddy's money can't buy you a pass."

"At least I know who my Dad is."

"What did you just say?" Red flashed in front of my eyes and heat burned at my throat.

"Lyssa, leave it."

Sam stepped between us before I floored her with my curled fist. I glared at her smug face over his shoulder, and then spun away.

"Is nothing private around here?" I fumed the second I was out of earshot. "How could she possibly know I'm adopted?"

Sam shook his head.

"No idea. But I know she's not worth it."

"He's right," Kelsey said. "Don't let her get under your skin. You know that's what she wants."

"Easy for you to say," I said, but of course they were right. I'd made it through the entire year – somehow – and I wasn't going to do anything to get myself kicked out now. Assuming I hadn't flunked any major exams.

Despite being exhausted from an entire week of relentless exams, when night finally came, I couldn't sleep. I spent a couple of hours tossing and turning before a light came on across the room. Kelsey rolled over, hand still on her lamp, and looked at me through bleary eyes.

"Sorry, I didn't mean to disturb you."

She sat up and brushed her hair out of her eyes.

"That's okay. What's wrong?"

What *was* wrong? Something, that was for sure. I shook my head.

"I don't know. I need to take a walk."

"Around the castle, in the middle of the night?"

"Nope," I said, swinging my legs over the side of the bed and pulling on some warm clothes as I made up my mind. "I'm going to the gryff barn."

"Lyssa, that's crazy!"

"Tell me something I don't know." So much for not doing anything to get myself kicked out. "I need to see Stormclaw. I can't explain it."

"Can't it wait until morning?" Kelsey pleaded. "We'll find a professor to escort us out there."

"Nope." I pulled on my boots, and hunted around the room quickly for my heavy cloak. "What are you doing?"

Kelsey had climbed out of her bed and was pulling on her boots, too.

"Well, isn't it obvious? I'm coming with you."

Chapter Twenty-One

Kelsey wouldn't be persuaded to stay behind, so ten minutes later we were both creeping out through the large door at the front of the academy, and into the chilly night air. She shivered, wrapping her cloak more tightly around her.

"Let's just be quick, okay?"

"Sure. We'll just check on him, then go back to bed."

I was already having second thoughts about coming out here. Kelsey was right: this was crazy. We could both be expelled for being out tonight. Just a quick peek at Stormclaw, and then I'd go back to bed. We were halfway there already, it seemed silly to turn around and go back now.

"Did you hear that?" Kelsey hissed.

"Hear what?" I hissed back, looking around us, but all I could see was darkness and shadows under the waning moon. I froze, straining my ears, but the only sounds in the night air were my own rapid breathing and pounding heart. I caught movement in my periphery, and spun, looking wildly around me until my eyes rested on the tree branch disturbed by the wind.

"Forget it," Kelsey said, eyeing the branch. "Let's just get moving."

We were approaching the greenhouses when she froze again, grabbing hold of my cloak to stop me in my tracks. She pressed a finger to her lips and spun me around.

"You're both getting expelled for this."

"Felicity!" There was no mistaking the gloating look on the girl's face under the pale moonlight.

"I knew you were up to something, sneaking around the castle at night. Just wait until I tell Professor Talendale, he'll have you out of here by morning." She looked me up and down. "It's about time. You should never have been allowed in here to start with."

Kelsey's grip on my wrist tightened, her nails biting into my skin.

"Ow! Watch it! Don't worry about this airhead, she can't tell Professor Talendale about us being out here without admitting to being out here herself."

But Kelsey wasn't looking at Felicity – she was looking over her shoulder, and her face had gone sheet white.

"The guards, Lyssa – for the Beathanian. They're gone!"

"What?" My eyes widened. "The Beathanian! Come on!"

I shoved past Felicity and raced for the greenhouse, all thoughts of expelled firmly from my mind. If anything happened to that plant, Keira and Ethan and Professor Alden, they could all die.

"Stop!" Felicity shouted, and a sudden gust of air took my legs from under me. I hit the ground hard and rolled with a grunt.

"You–"

Another gust of air ripped the words from my lips, and Felicity stood, hand outstretched, staring down at me.

"I'm going to enjoy this," she said, with a twisted smile as she advanced on me. But at the last moment she spun, and directed her blast of air at Kelsey, tossing her to the ground as easily as she'd tossed me. As soon as her back was turned I started conjuring a fireball… but I couldn't bring myself to throw it. She could get hurt, seriously hurt, and no matter what a vindictive little airhead she was, she didn't deserve to be burned. But that didn't mean I had to tell *her* that.

"Leave her alone, Felicity," I said, getting to my feet and letting the fireball hover in the air in front of us. She spun back to me, hand raised and her face distorted in a snarl. Kelsey stayed on the floor.

"Are you okay? I called, but her only answer was a grunt. After a moment she staggered to her feet, looking dazed. My head snapped back to Felicity and I edged the ball towards her.

"You wouldn't dare!"

"Wouldn't I? Like you said, I'm already expelled for being out here. What've I got to lose?"

Felicity backed away, blanching. Behind her, in the treeline, something moved.

"Look out!" I shouted, but I was much too late. The creature lunged out of the shadows, throwing itself at her and knocking her to the ground in a shadowy tangle of arms and legs. I caught only a glimpse of it mid-air, but it looked human. Then the rancid stench reached me, and I knew it couldn't be. Nothing human could smell that vile. I gagged, choking on the heavy scent I'd smelled twice before – in the Unhallowed Grove, and then again in the hallways on Halloween. But this time, I knew what it was. What I could smell was rotting flesh. And death.

I aimed my palm at the floating fireball, and with a grunt I launched it through the air, towards the grappling pair. As it neared them, I could see Felicity sprawled on the floor, and poised above her was the unmistakable rotting face of a dead man. My guts churned, trying to reject my dinner, but I swallowed hard and pushed the fireball forwards again. The creature squealed in panic and drew back, away from Felicity. Now was my chance. With a shout, I threw the ball into its exposed shirt, and the creature gave a feral moan of pain. The tattered remains of its shirt started to burn, but under the fabric, the dead man's skin was barely scorched. I wasn't strong enough on my own.

"Kelsey!" I shouted, throwing another fireball, and another. Each one hit its mark, leaving a pattern of scorch marks across the rotting flesh, and the creature began to back away from Felicity's unmoving body. But if it escaped into the forest, there was no telling when it would strike again. Or if it would kill next time. We couldn't let it escape.

A fireball struck its back and the creature cried out again. My eyes snapped to Kelsey, whose hand was outstretched. She gave me a grim nod. I stretched my hand out again and we attacked the dead man from both sides, yet still it was barely having an impact. Our fire just couldn't find any purchase to spread.

"Hit him again." The voice came from the floor. Felicity had propped herself up, one hand gripping her shoulder, but the other shakily outstretched. "On three."

"One," I conjured a ball up between both palms, focussing all of my waning energy into it.

"Two," Kelsey called, and I shoved my ball forwards, letting it merge with hers, mid-air.

"Three!" We flung the massive ball together and it smashed into the dead man's chest with a thud I could feel from where I stood. Before it could go out, a breeze started flickering at its edges, fanning the flames and spreading over the creature until it was wreathed in flames, arms flailing and a horrible, inhuman screech filled the night air. His tattered clothing went up, and with one last groan, he slid to the floor, smouldering, and was still.

Another moan sounded, and Felicity sunk back to the floor.

"She's okay," Kelsey called out, dropping to the ground beside her. "Check on the plant!"

My stomach clenched. The plant! I'd forgotten all about it in the chaos. But someone had raised that man from the dead, and lured the guards away, and I had to get to the plant before they did.

I hurried to the greenhouse and as I did, I caught a glimpse of a shadow, and something slipping in through the door. Taking a deep breath, I conjured another ball of fire in my hand, and slipped through the door behind it. I looked around, ready to attack, and saw–

"Toby!"

I gasped in relief and shook my head as the hammering in my chest subsided. That damned cat was going to be the death of me. What the hell was he doing, skulking around out here in the dark? It didn't matter. I brushed past him, careful to avoid taking a set of claws to my leg.

"Well?" Kelsey gasped, bracing herself in the doorway and throwing a glance back to Felicity. I directed my fire ball to hover over the Beathanian plant's bench and got a good look at it under the flickering light. Relief flooded through me.

"It's still here," I said. It looked exactly the same as it had that afternoon. "It's okay, thank God, it's—"

I broke off as a thud sounded behind me. I spun around, and my eyes widened as they took in the scene. Kelsey was in a crumped heap on the floor, and a shadowy figure stood outlined behind her.

"Who… who are you?" I stammered, looking down at my friend. "What did you do to her?"

"She'll be fine. I just didn't want us to be disturbed." The man stepped out of the shadows, and the light flickered across his gaunt, unfamiliar face. "I'm sorry, where are my manners? My name is Raphael, but you know me as Toby."

My fireball flicked and blinked out of existence. The man clicked his fingers, and another appeared in its place. I paid it no attention.

"You can't be. Toby's a wampus cat."

"Toby was a convenient disguise." Raphael stepped over Kelsey's unconscious body and advanced on me.

"Stay back!" I warned him. "I won't let you destroy this plant."

"Come now, Lyssa, if I wanted to hurt you, you'd be like your friends. But I will have that plant. I destroyed the others, but this one has proved surprisingly resilient. I'll put an end to that tonight. I've come too far to let one little plant come between me and my goals."

"You raised him," I said. "The dead man in the forest. That was you." I stared at him in horror as it sunk in. "And in the grove, and the hallways at Halloween. Everywhere I smelt it, I saw Toby."

"Yes, well, I couldn't very well risk you disturbing my little experiment and getting hurt, could I?"

"You didn't have any problem hurting other people," I said, edging to one side and trying to circle round to the door. Raphael stepped too, keeping himself between me and the only way out.

"But don't you see?" He smiled, his teeth flashing white in the flickering light of his fireball. "I did all of that *for* you."

"For me?" None of this was making any sense. I needed to get away from this lunatic, back to the castle. I needed one of the professors. Even Atherton would do right now.

"Don't sound so surprised. Surely, you must have suspected?" he said, the smile tugging at the corners of his mouth like he was teasing me with a riddle. When I didn't answer, he continued, "The Keria girl was standing between you and a spot on the team. I removed her. And when I heard what that dragon rider tried with you…"

His lip curled into a snarl and his fireball doubled in size before he composed himself. "Well, I could hardly allow him to go unpunished, could I? The professor needn't have got hurt, but she insisted on trying to stop me with these wretched plants. Of course, she's the only one who knows how to harvest the seeds, so with her out of the way, I was free to carry on. Just as soon as my creature regained his strength."

"And Felicity?" I said, groping for a way to keep him talking as I backed away, towards one of the tall windows at the rear of the greenhouse. He laughed.

"She was a bonus. But I certainly couldn't have her getting you expelled now, could I?"

"Why not? I don't understand!"

He grinned, like it was all some grand secret.

"You will. One day. But right now, we need to have a little chat. Right after I destroy that last plant."

"Down there, by the greenhouse!" The voice sounded distantly, and as I looked through the tinted glass, I saw a handful of floating fireballs, growing larger as they got closer. Raphael whipped his head round with a snarl. Without another word, he shrank into the form of a ginger cat, opened a small portal, and darted through it.

Chapter Twenty-Two

I'd never been so glad to be inside Professor Talendale's office. Actually, I'd never been glad to be inside his office at all, given that invariably I was having a shit tonne of bad news dumped on me. But tonight was an exception, and I could not have been happier to be inside the large, creepy, and oddly-animated chamber.

I was slumped in a chair, aching head to toe – an all too familiar side effect of overusing my powers – and the professor was regarding me from the other side of his living desk.

"Professor, is there any news about–"

He raised his eyebrows and I fell silent, swallowing the rest of my question. I hadn't seen Kelsey or Felicity since the professors had found us out by the greenhouses. I might not have been Felicity's biggest fan – okay, that was an understatement – but when it came down to it, she'd really come through for us. I hoped she was okay.

The professor exhaled heavily and leaned back in his seat.

"Ms Eldridge, what you did tonight is enough to get you expelled from Dragondale, and have your magic permanently bound."

"I know, Professor, but I–"

He raised a hand and I clamped my mouth shut again, staring down at my mud-covered boots.

"However, you are also the reason that Raphael and his abomination were stopped, and we can't very well expel the hero of Dragondale, can we?"

I jerked my head up; he had a barest hint of a smile crinkling round the edges of his mouth.

"I'm not getting expelled?"

"Not this time. Now, I imagine you have a lot of questions about what happened tonight. Let me start with what I imagine is the first of them. Both Miss Winters and Miss Hutton are in the medical wing and recovering well. Miss Hutton was bitten, but Professor Sumner seems to think the Beathanian plant will be ready for harvesting in the morning, and so she and the other victims should make full recoveries in the next couple of days."

I nodded, taking a moment to let the information sink in. Kelsey and Felicity were okay. And Keira and Ethan and Professor Ellerby, they were all going to be fine, too. It would have been a different story if we hadn't gotten to that plant first.

"Thank you, Professor."

"You have other questions?"

I nodded again – I had about a hundred. I didn't think his good will would extent to a hundred questions though, so I started with the most important.

"Toby – I mean, Raphael – who is he, really?"

"I believe you know about skin walkers?" he said, and his eyes seemed to pin me to the spot as I recalled mine and Sam's ill-fated attempts to transform ourselves, and my fluffy tail. "Very little happens inside these walls of which I am not aware, Ms Eldridge."

"Yes, Professor," I answered his question, and tried to quell the unsettling sensation squirming in my stomach.

"Unfortunately, Toby was one of those few things that slipped past my notice. I believed him – as did we all – to be a wampus cat. It came as a great surprise to me to learn his true identity tonight. Not least because Raphael is no stranger to me. He once attended this academy, many years ago."

"He did?" I was leaning forward on my seat without realising it. "What happened?"

"He was an excellent pupil. He excelled in many of his classes, some say he was one of the brightest students Dragondale has ever known."

"And you?" I asked, breathlessly.

"I, Ms Eldridge, believe that there is more to excellence than merely being academically gifted. Raphael frequently clashed with his classmates; often he could be found at the centre of this or that altercation. Of course, it was not always that way. When he first arrived at Dragondale he showed great promise, his attitude was excellent. Indeed, he had every mark of becoming a great druid one day."

He leaned back in his seat again, looking mournful.

"We may never know what changed him, but almost overnight he became different. Surly. More aggressive. Such a shame. He graduated, though there are those of us who felt he should not have, that he was a danger to the magical community."

"Why?" The single word slipped from my lips without permission. Talendale cleared his throat.

"Well, I don't think we need get into that. But there have been rumours about his... activities since graduation. Suffice to say, young lady, that you had a very lucky escape this evening."

His voice had turned stern again and I tried my best to look repentant.

"I know, Professor. I'm sorry."

"Hm, yes, I'm sure you are," he said, sounding anything but.

"What about... what about that... thing he raised? Is it dead now? How did he do that?"

The professor stroked his chin.

"So many questions. There are many branches of magic, as you will learn – some more frowned upon than others. Necromancy is one of those branches. Indeed, there are very few places one can even learn such magics."

"But one of them is here," I blurted.

"No, not at all." Professor Talendale's voice sharpened. "We would never permit such dark magic to be practiced inside our hallowed walls, let alone encourage it."

I vividly recalled the book I found in the library, the book on necromancy that wasn't as covered in dust as the other books. Talendale watched me closely – he was right, there was very little he missed.

"There are some here who do study it," he said, "in order to learn how best to combat its effects. And well it is too – without such studies we would not know the proper way to counter the effects of Raphael's abomination, nor how to ensure it is laid to rest, once and for all."

"Then… it is dead?"

The professor inclined his head.

"It is."

"What about Toby – Raphael – whoever. What if he just comes back and raises more of them? What if–"

I realised my voice was bordering on hysterical and sucked in a deep breath. The thought of that creature coming near me, biting me, its rotten teeth sinking into my flesh... I'd been so close to it, so many times.

"That won't happen, dear," Talendale said, in a tone that was almost kindly, but his face was as impassive as always. "The academy carefully monitors who is permitted to portal in and out of its grounds. We granted Toby special permissions as a mascot of Dragondale, but those permissions have been revoked, and as himself, Raphael never had dispensation to portal into the academy. He will no longer be able to cross our threshold without using the main gate, and I assure you, that shall not happen. In fact, I have no doubt that he shall be apprehended in the very near future. Put him from your mind."

If only it was that simple.

"He said some things."

"Oh?"

"He said he chose his victims to protect me, and that he meant me no harm. Why would he say that?"

"Interesting. Very interesting." The professor rose to his feet and paced the cold stone floor. My eyes flickered as they followed him. Abruptly, he stopped and turned to look out of the window.

"I fear that must remain a mystery, for now, at least. Perhaps he was aware of your potential – your control of opposing elements. Perhaps he saw something of himself in you. Regardless, he will no longer bother you. And I believe you have bigger things with which to concern yourself."

I frowned, wondering if maybe the lack of sleep was catching up with me, because nothing more important than the walking dead and a mysterious outcast benefactor came to mind.

"I do?"

"There is a certain game that was postponed until the threat was dealt with. That threat has now been removed, but I fear young Keira will not be up to taking her position. This will be your debut game, will it not?"

I stared at him with open mouth.

"This academy has a noble history in the sport of Itealta, Ms Eldridge. I trust you will not let us down."

Chapter Twenty-Three

I was excused from my lessons for the next two days, along with all of the other riders on the four Itealta teams. Logan was brutal in training, determined to get us in shape for the game. Our training sessions were enough to keep Madam Leechinton busy – which she wasn't thrilled about, while she was busily coaxing Keira, Felcitiy, Ethan and Professor Ellebry through their recovery. Eventually, after Josh had made three trips to the hospital wing inside an hour, she threatened to leave any more of our injured players to heal naturally, and Logan eased up on us a little – which was to say the sessions were only horrific, as opposed to torturous.

By the time the afternoon of the match came around, I was pretty sure we were all of the verge of mutiny. Logan caught up with us in the main hall, just as I was about to tuck into an indulgently unhealthy burger and fries. If ever there was a time for comfort food, this was it.

"Alright team," Logan said, pulling out a chair and setting a tray with a single apple on it on the table in front of him. "It's our first – our only – game this season, so I don't need to tell you how important it is. Earth and Water are going to play before us, and the winner of the

Itealta cup is going to be determined entirely on goals scored."

There were a couple of groans from round the table. I looked around the glum faces.

"What? Why is that bad?"

"Air have won the cup for the last four years running," Josh said. He slumped forward onto the table and buried his head in his arms. "We're screwed."

Logan aimed his hand at the small circle of Josh's head visible above his arms.

"That's quitter talk. They won't need to defeat us out there if you're already defeated in here." He switched his attention to me as Josh rubbed the back of his head ruefully. "We might have the toughest game, but that just means we'll have all the more glory when we beat them. Our manoeuvres are tighter than they've ever been, and we've got a secret weapon: Stormclaw."

Great. No pressure, then. I shoved my burger and fries aside, untouched.

"That's the spirit," Logan said. "Healthy body, healthy mind."

He tossed me his apple. I looked at it then for a second then dropped it onto the table. It was even less appealing than the hot food.

"Now, I know it's yours and Stormclaw's first game, but he was bred for this. And I made you first reserve for a reason. I wouldn't be letting you play if I didn't have complete confidence in you both."

Yeah, and that was the problem. What if I fell fifty feet with the whole academy watching? Worse, what if I let the team down?

"Uh, do you get to bring on a replacement if I fall to my death?"

He clapped me on the shoulder with a laugh.

"You've kept your sense of humour, I like that."

"Humour. Right," I muttered.

The main hall emptied around us as the rest of the students went outside to watch the first game.

"Right, gather round," Logan said, as an Earth hurried out of the room, leaving only our table occupied. "Time for one last run through of our tactics."

Logan's run through took nearly an hour, leaving us with just over sixty minutes to get our gryffs warmed up and down to the pitch. I was the last to leave, after taking my tray of congealed food back to the kitchen mage.

"Good luck, Lyssa," he said. "Not that you'll need it."

"Thanks," I muttered, and headed out of the hall and almost walked straight into the rest of my team clustered around a shrunken figure in a red cloak.

"Keira!" I reached forward and embraced her gently, worried I might break her; she looked so pale and fragile. "Shouldn't you still be in the hospital wing?"

"We convinced old Leech that it would help our recovery if we got outside for a while. Me and that Air girl. And I couldn't miss the game, could I?"

I felt a pang of guilt; I was riding in Keira's spot on the team. She must've seen it on my face, because she met my eye with a smile.

"I can't think of anyone better to ride my position while I'm not up to it. But don't pay attention to what any of these boneheads tell you."

Logan puffed up with mock indignation and she flipped him off causally.

"They'll expect you to be everywhere at once, but you're a winger – your place is on the wing. Your opposite number on the Air team, Anika Mahto, is wicked fast and if you're not guarding that flank, she'll be right up there before you know it, ready for their centre to offload for a fast goal. She's their best player, and no matter what anyone tells you, she's your only priority."

With this, she cocked an eyebrow at Logan, as though daring him to correct her.

"She's got a point," he conceded. "Mahto's a real threat – but just don't lose sight of the rest of the game. Teams win games, not individuals."

"Okay! Can you please all stop giving me advice, before my head explodes?"

"Just one more thing," Keira said with a smile.

"What?"

"Have fun."

Like that was going to happen. My stomach had been possessed by a pile of wrestling snakes and I could barely put one foot in front of the other as I traipsed down to Stormclaw's stall with all the enthusiasm of a condemned woman walking to the gallows. By the time I reached the barn, I was so busy staring at the ground and wishing it would open up and swallow me that I almost walked straight into her.

"Watch where you're going, Charity."

"Felicity. Look, I'm really busy, I've got to get Stormclaw warmed up. If you've come to say thanks there's really no—"

"Hardly." She looked like she had a bad taste in her mouth, but maybe it was just her own bitterness. "What on earth would I have to thank you for?"

"Um, I don't know, saving your life?"

She closed the gap between us and hissed at me.

"That is *not* what happened, and if that's what you've been going around telling everyone, then you're going to be sorry. And even if you had help me in some small way, I wouldn't have been in danger in the first place if you hadn't been breaking rules, so make sure you tell them *that*."

"Relax," I said, and tried to force the muscles in my shoulders to follow my own advice, without much success. Felicity was trying my patience. "I haven't been talking to anyone. Literally. Logan's training regime has been brutal. Speaking of which, I've got a game to win, so if you don't mind…"

She didn't move, so I brushed past her.

"Wait!"

I turned around with a sigh.

"What, Felicity?"

"Forget it. Go get ready for your game – you're going to need all the practice you can get, going up against Mahto."

She sneered, then turned and hobbled away. I stalked into the barn, snatched up Stormclaw's headcollar and let myself into his stall, fuming the whole while.

"The gall of her," I snapped as I clipped Stormclaw's bridle on. "I *did* save her life, and she knows it. Should have just let the zombie eat her."

"That's some pep talk."

I jumped, and shoved my head over the stall door to see Logan standing in the aisle with his gryff, Dartalon, waiting patiently at his shoulder.

"Are you ready?"

"I just need to get Stormclaw's saddle on."

"Good. Join us in the paddock as soon as you're ready," he said, and started to lead his gryff towards the exit. "And Lyssa? That airhead was just trying to psyche you out. Don't let her get under your skin."

That was easier said than done, but I tried to put her out of my mind, for now at least. Getting on a gryff with less than perfect concentration was likely to end up with a trip to the hospital wing, and I doubted Madam Leechington would have time to get me patched up before the match started now.

I grabbed Stormclaw's saddle from its rack and slid it onto his back, taking care not to trap any of his feathers, or brush any of his hairs the wrong way. Watching out for his front claws, one of which was impatiently scratching at the floor in his stall, I ducked under his belly and tightened the girth strap. The last thing I wanted was the saddle to slip and leave me clinging to my mount's underside like some sort of circus monkey.

"Alright, boy," I said, stroking his glistening neck feathers and working a dead one loose. "This is our big moment. Just... don't drop me, okay?"

He tossed his head, ruffling his plumage and puffing out his chest.

"Come on, then, let's go."

I slipped my hand into his head collar, and led him from his stall into the paddock. The rest of the team were already out and warming up, and in the distance a cheer went up, as either Earth or Water scored a goal. A shiver ran through me, raising goosebumps on my arms. In a short while, their game would end, and then it would be us the crowd were cheering. One game to determine the winners of the cup: it was all or nothing.

I drew in a deep breath and blew it out slowly, then scrambled up into the saddle. I gave Stormclaw a quick scratch on his shoulders, then clenched my calf muscles. He took off at a slow lope, circling the perimeter of the paddock. I let him do his own thing for a while, stretching out his muscles and shaking out his wings, while I loosened off my own muscles and shook the fear from my mind. His scent filled my nostrils as we cantered round in his odd gait, feeling the pump of each one of his legs driving us forward. His wings flexed on either side as the wind whistled through his flight feathers. My hips relaxed and my legs stretched downwards, taking up the contact against his warm, feather-covered body. It felt good to be back on the gryff, the one place I felt truly at home. Forget the game, forget the cup, forget the whole academy: *this* was what I was born to do.

Except it wasn't quite that easy to forget, I admitted wryly to myself, after half a dozen blissful laps. Reluctantly, I picked up the reins and guided him over to where the rest of the team were tossing a ball around. If I wanted to keep riding, it'd probably be a good idea to check I hadn't forgotten how to catch a ball without breaking any fingers.

Chapter Twenty-Four

And please show your appreciation as the Fire team enter the field!"

The voice of the commentator rang in my ears, muffled only slightly by the helmet strapped to my head. The rest of team trotted out in front of me, while the commentators – Finn, from Earth element, and Adam from Water – announced them to the gathered crowd.

"After a one-one draw between Earth and Water, there is everything to play for. If the winning team score two or more goals, they will take the cup for this year."

"First up is Logan Walsh, riding Dartalon, and from the look on his face, he knows what's at stake. This is his second-year riding on the team, and his first time captaining it. He'll be playing centre by the looks of it today. Excellent rider."

"You're not wrong, Finn," Adam said. "It's a real shame his team hasn't had more chances to show us what they're made of. And here we have Josh Saunders, riding Riverquil in the right attack position, and Darren Wilcox on Lightning riding left attack."

"Next we have the two defenders, Caleb Armstrong on Swiftsky and Liu Zung on Ironclaw. This will be

Zung's third and final season and she'll be wanting to make it a good one."

"Every team needs a keeper, and here comes theirs – it's Seb Foster riding Blackstar, and he's really got something to prove today after last season's performance."

"He has, indeed. Some people have questioned Walsh's decision to keep him on the team – will he redeem himself this afternoon?"

"And last but not least, we have the two outriders. Taking left wing is Mason Fuller on Ghost – last season was plagued by lameness, Finn, let's hope the long rest has done his gryff some good."

"And there she is, Adam, the one everyone's been talking about. Lyssa Eldridge. A first year, some would say an outsider, raised away from the druidic world."

"That's right, Finn, she hadn't even heard of Itealta this time last year. Let's hope she's had time to learn the rules."

I shot a glare at the commentary box; was this guy for real? From the looks on some of my teammates' faces, I was sure I hadn't been the only one who'd caught his snarky tone. We'd show him.

"Come on, Stormclaw," I muttered as the rest of the team took to the air, and Logan led us on a circuit past the spectators in stands.

"But it's not just Eldridge that will be setting tongues wagging today. Some of you might recognise her mount – that's Stormclaw she's riding. Many a student here can attest to his fiery nature."

"Indeed they can," Adam agreed. "Will he prove too much for his novice rider?"

Novice indeed! I tucked my chin and fought the urge to cut away from the flyby and give Adam a very personal demonstration of just how fiery my boy could be when someone rubbed him the wrong way. The team finished their loop of the pitch and came down to land in centre of the field. I took Stormclaw down with them, bringing him to a halt at the end of the semi-circle the team had formed.

"And here come the Air team," Adam announced, his amplified voice bouncing around the arena. "Undoubtedly the favourites for this particular match."

"But let's not forget," Finn added brightly, "Everyone loves an underdog."

I leaned sideways in my saddle towards Mason.

"Did he just call me a dog?"

Mason sniggered. The commentators carried on announcing the Air team – captain Mark Bolton, then Lindsay Bartlett and Noah Howell, but I'd stopped listening. The crowd were cheering in the stands, which accommodated every student from the academy and had space to spare. They ran round the entire rectangular grass-covered pitch, and reached up fifty foot in the air. The pitch itself was long and wide, and bore eight rocky platforms. At either end was a vertical hoop atop a long metal pole, big enough that the ball would pass through it, but small enough that it made for a tricky shot when you were riding a creature straight out of mythology through the skies.

The umpire – Professor Alden, mounted on a pure white gryff wearing a red ribbon around her chest and holding the Itealta ball in one hand – blew her whistle, the sound echoing round the arena.

"Starting positions!" she called.

I nudged Stormclaw and we flew up onto the platform at the far right and centre of the field, facing our hoop. Mahto on her impressive chestnut gryff landed next to us. It was the first time I'd seen her up close. I just hoped that she wasn't as good as everyone said. She shot me a smile, her brown eyes sparkling with excitement, and she stretched her hand out to me.

"Looking forward to trouncing you, Eldridge."

I reached over and shook her hand with a grin.

"Hope your game is as good as your mouth, Mahto."

Alden blew her whistle again, and threw the ball up in the air. I was still watching to see where it would land when Mahto launched herself forward, her gryff leaping easily from the rock.

"Dammit," I muttered, and pressed my hands against Stormclaw. He leapt into the air after the chestnut gryff, a full two lengths behind.

"And Mahto is off to a flying start," Finn said. "She doesn't miss a trick."

"She certainly doesn't, Finn. Eldridge will have to get up earlier in the morning if she wants to get the drop on her more experienced opposite number."

I gritted my teeth and shook his voice from my head, just as Mahto leaned out of her saddle and snatched up the ball from the floor. Her gryff kicked off the ground back into the air, flying straight for their hoop.

"Come on, Stormclaw!" I felt his wings beat harder and we rocketed through the sky after them, but Logan was already alongside her, reaching out with both hands to rip the ball from her.

"Oh! And that was an impressive take by Logan Walsh for Fire. Mahto does not look happy, but he's already offloaded the ball."

"Armstrong. Now Fuller. To Zung, and– What an interception that was, Mahto is unstoppable today!"

"Air are in possession. Bartlett. Howell. Here comes Mahto on the wing, she's got the ball, she's racing towards the hoop, can Foster get there in time to stop her? No, he can't! Goal!"

"Goal to Air team, well done Mahto. What an excellent piece of riding."

I gritted my teeth and turned Stormclaw back to our plinth. It *had* been an excellent piece of riding, but we were supposed to be the ones to stop her, and we'd been two lengths behind. Again. Mahto landed beside us, grinning widely, her cheeks flushed with exhilaration.

I nodded to her, then twisted round in my saddle, watching Alden bringing the ball into the centre of the pitch. I wasn't going to be caught napping this time. I relaxed my shoulders, and the moment the ball left her hand, clenched my calves against Stormclaw and pushed my hands forward. He threw himself forward, a half length in front of Mahto. I caught a glimpse of the surprise on her face and smiled grimly to myself as I put us into a dive, right down to the ball. Forget staying on the wing; if Mahto wasn't going to do that, then I couldn't afford to, either.

Stormclaw's talons touched the ground, and a split second later, his hooves thudded behind them. I gripped the saddle horn and leaned right down, stretching out my fingertips, and– Dammit! A hand grabbed the ball, and I looked up into Mahto's grinning face as her gryff climbed back into the air.

"An impressive steal by Mahto," Adam said. "Just goes to show that having the fastest gryff doesn't count for everything."

I barely even heard the criticism as I urged Stormclaw after Mahto, but by the time I'd reached her, she'd already tossed the ball to one of her teammates. Caleb was hot on his tail, so I eased Stormclaw back and stuck close to Mahto as she moved back out onto the wing. If I couldn't grab the ball before her, maybe I could use our greater speed to keep her away from it.

She swung inwards from the wing as the ball came down the centre of the pitch and I raced after her.

"Down!" I called to Stormclaw, ducking low against his neck as we flew right under Mahto, narrowly avoiding her mount's talons. I saw the look of confusion on her face as we disappeared from view, and then we were rising up on her inside, blocking her from getting to the rest of her team.

"Morley has possession for Air, but Fire have him cut off from the hoop. He's looking for Mahto – where is Mahto?"

Mahto wheeled away in a sharp circle, but rather than sticking with her and going round her outside, I pulled Stormclaw in the opposite direction, mirroring her movement and keeping myself between her and the game. She dove at the ground and we followed. She hadn't seen the ball. With a flash of intuition I knew exactly what she was planning – springboarding off the ground and hoping to use her superior riding skills to shake me. I pulled Stormclaw up a few feet before she landed, and rose up again with her, still side by side with her chestnut beast. She shot me a glare of frustration, but I didn't respond, too focussed on anticipating her gryff's movements.

"It looks like Eldridge has got Mahto's number," Finn announced, and I couldn't help but notice he sounded just a little impressed. A fierce stab of pride ran through me. "She's neutralised Air's best weapon."

"She'll have to learn a few new tricks if she hopes to keep it up."

"Fumble by Air! Loose ball on the floor, both captains are diving down for it."

"Bolton has grabbed the ball for Air, he's got his eyes on the hoop, but Logan isn't going to let him past, he's between him and the hoop and he's riding straight at him. They're going to collide…"

"Oooh! So close, they miss each other by a feather, and it looks like Bolton has lost his balance! Fuller's coming up on his inside for Fire, and look out, here comes Wilcox… Can he… Yes! Wilcox has snatched the ball from him! What an excellent execution of the liotus manoeuvre!"

"Logan. Saunders. Back to Logan, he's approaching the hoop...

"He shoots... he scores! A fantastic equaliser for Fire. One all as we head into half time."

By the time Alden blew her whistle to signal half-time, both our mounts were covered in a sheen of sweat, but Mahto hadn't managed to slip past me. I landed at our end of the pitch with the rest of my team, hopping off Stormclaw's back and leading him over to one of the buckets of water someone had brought out, then grabbing a bottle for myself. Blocking Mahto was taking it out of us both.

"Excellent work, Lyssa," Logan said, clapping me on the back so hard I choked on my water. "If you can keep Mahto out of the game, we might just beat them."

He turned to Darren.

"Great job on the liotus. We're got them on the run now. Watch your flanks and don't give them the chance to slip through us. We've got this! Come on!"

We cheered loudly, and vaulted back onto our gryffs, then circled them back round to our plinths. Mahto was already waiting for me, watching me with new respect.

"Nice riding," she acknowledged curtly.

"You, too," I said, and meant it.

The whistle blew and the ball flew up into the air, and the pair of us took off as one. I raced the length of the field alongside her, forcing her to fly wide towards the crowd and blocking her from the action. I could feel Stormclaw flying more slowly beneath me; this was taking a toll on him. For a moment I thought Mahto's beast would beat us purely on fitness, but then I spotted his neck stretching just a little less as he flew; a sure sign he was tiring, too.

I barely registered the rest of the game as I faced-off against the chestnut gryff, trying to outsmart his more experienced rider at every turn. Even the commentators' voices were blotted out as I focussed every ounce of my attention on the pair, spinning and twisting, ducking down and rising back up again in some elaborate ballet of the skies. Occasionally we drifted closer to the crowds and their 'oohs' and 'aahhs' punched through my laser focus, and then it was just me and Mahto again, locked in our aerial dance. With just five minutes left in the game, neither side had scored again, and Mahto had failed at every attempt to break through my block. Maybe it made me complacent.

"She's done it!" Adam roared. "Mahto has broken through Eldridge's wall and she is going after the ball!"

She had. It took my brain a moment to catch up – she'd just used my own move against me and ducked right under us – and by the time it had, she was already three lengths ahead of us.

"Dammit! Come on, Stormclaw! One last push!"

I urged him forwards with everything I had, and I felt him dig deep and respond. Suddenly Mahto was only two lengths ahead of me, then one, then I was passing her and diving at the ball.

"Just look at that, Adam. Eldridge is streaking across the pitch, I've never seen anyone move so fast, and she's got her eyes on the prize!"

As Stormclaw's talons touched down, I threw myself sideways from the saddle, hooking my right knee behind the saddlehorn and stretching right down for the ball. My fingers clenched around its metal handle and Stormclaw's hooves thumped into the ground, almost throwing me from the saddle, and then he was springing back into the air. The movement slung me back into my saddle and we were racing through the skies again. Both my hands were gripping the ball like my life depended on it and I steered Stormclaw with just my body.

"What a pick-up! Have you ever seen anything like it?" Finn shouted. "We're into the final seconds of the game. Go on, Eldridge!"

The other riders blurred in my periphery as we raced past them, ducking this way and that to keep out of their reach. And there is was, right ahead of me. The hoop.

"Come on, Stormclaw!" I screamed. "Go. Go!"

We raced the other riders and the clock, bearing down on the hoop. It was now or never.

I lifted the ball up, sucked in a hasty breath, and threw it with all my strength. Time seemed to slow down as it soared through the air towards the hoop. The whole arena fell silent as we watched the ball.

"Goal!" screamed Finn. "She's done it, the ball is through the hoop, she's scored!"

Alden's whistle sounded in three long blasts.

"The match is over! Fire two, Air one, Fire win, Fire take the cup!"

Chapter Twenty-Five

The celebrations continued long into the night, though truth be told I couldn't remember anything that happened much past nine. I did recall half of Fire element carrying me back to our common room on their shoulders, and the other half passing the cup around, cheering wildly.

When I woke the following morning, I felt like I'd been hit by a dragon. There wasn't a single muscle in my body that wasn't aching, and I had a few dozen fresh bruises – though whether those were from the match, or the afterparty, I couldn't have said.

"Come on, Lyssa, let's go!"

I stretched on my bed and yawned loudly, rolling my head to one side to squint at Kelsey through bleary eyes.

"Hurry up!"

She tossed some clothes in my direction.

"Where's the fire?" I mumbled.

"We're getting our exam results. Come *on*!"

I was instantly wide awake, a flutter on panic stirring in my stomach.

"That's today?"

"Yes! They're handing them out first thing at breakfast, and if you don't get a move on, we're going to be late."

"Alright, I'm up, I'm up."

It was a couple of minutes until I was, in fact, up and dressed, by which time Kelsey was bouncing from foot to foot in front of the door.

"Don't know what you're in such a hurry for," I grumbled. "We already know you passed everything."

She gave me a sympathetic smile.

"I'm sure you did fine. You've been studying really hard and, anyway," she paused to yank open the door. "There's no point in putting it off."

I bowed to her superior wisdom and followed her down the corridor to the common room. Sam grinned when he saw us.

"I was starting to think you'd gone without me. Figured maybe the suspense got too much for you."

Had everyone known about this other than me? I kept my thoughts to myself, because looking round the common room at the anxious pack of students, it was clear that everyone *had* known. Actually, now that I thought about it, I did sort of recall the professors announcing a date for the results. I'd just been too caught up in preparing for the match to pay it much attention. I paused mid-step as a thought struck me, and it took the others a moment to realise I'd stopped. They doubled back to me.

"If you're going to hurl," Sam said, "the bathroom's that way."

I shook my head. If we were getting our results this morning, then...

"Today's the last day of the semester, isn't it?"

"Hell, yeah," he said, stretching his arms out over his head with a grin. "A few more hours and then it's glorious freedom for two whole months."

Kelsey elbowed him in the ribs, giving him a disapproving look. His face fell.

"Oh, right. You, uh, you haven't seen your parents– I mean, your–"

"They're still my parents!" I cut him off, a little more harshly than I'd intended. "Sorry. I mean, yeah, it's going to be awkward, but they're still my family. They're the ones who raised me."

And lied about me being adopted for my entire life. Awkward didn't even begin to cover it. I forced a smile.

"Come on, we'd best go get our results."

"If you insist," Sam said with a sigh.

We carried on down to the main hall and queued up for our food – although how anyone could eat right now was beyond me; my toast sat untouched on my plate long after we'd reached our table. I took a sip from my coffee cup and glanced around – the professors were sitting at their table, and each head of element had a stack of envelopes in front of them.

The hall was awash with nervous chatter, but it wasn't until all the students were seated that the element heads each stood up, collected their envelopes, and approached their tables. I watched Professor Alden cross to us, the anxiety in my stomach growing with every step she took.

"You will shortly receive your exam results," Professor Talendale said, rising from his seat. "I urge you to remember: academic success is an honourable goal, but it is not the only one. So long as you strive to be a credit to the magical community, and abide by our laws, you shall have a place within these walls until you graduate. However long that may take you."

His eyes rested on one guy on the Water table, who was clearly a couple of years older than his companions, and a handful of chuckles sounded around the hall. The guy grinned and waved.

"This is my year!" the water element announced, to more chuckles.

"Indeed," the headmaster intoned, sounding deeply cynical. "Re-sits will be carried out at the end of summer, for those of you who require them. The rest of you shall be free to enjoy your break, but I urge you not to neglect your studies. First and second years, you have more study ahead of you, and I remind you that it will only get more intense from here. Third years: the magical community awaits your meaningful contribution, and I know you shall uphold the noble standing of Dragondale."

A few faces paled at his words, and I suspected mine might have been one of them. Another two years of even harder study… and then my whole future. What did druids even do for a living? But there'd be plenty of time to worry about that later. Like, much later.

"Once you have received your results and enjoyed your meals, you are free to begin your preparations to leave the academy. Portals will be opened from mid-day onwards. Your head of elements will be able to advise you on your assigned portal times."

He looked round – for what, I wasn't sure – and then gave a nod.

"Very well, then. Without further ado, we shall distribute your results."

He raised his arms, and the envelopes flew out of the professors' hands, racing down the lines of students and dropping to the table in front of them. One skidded to a halt in front of me, my name emblazoned on the front. I looked around; everyone else had theirs, too. A couple of people were flipping them over and opening them. I suddenly wasn't sure I wanted to know what was inside mine.

I heard a tearing sound from my left: Sam.

"It's like a bandaid, right? Best to just rip it off."

He gave us a lopsided grin then slid the paper out. His eyes scanned it – left to right, top to bottom – and then his lips curved into a relieved smile and he slumped forward onto the table, narrowly avoiding dunking his head in his cereals.

"Passed," he said into his arms. "Just about."

I looked to my right and Kelsey gave me a nervous smile.

"Okay, I'll go next."

She turned her envelope open, unstuck the flap, and eased the slip of paper out like she was defusing a bomb. As if she had anything to worry about. She sucked in a deep breath, let it out, and turned the sheet over.

"A pass," she said, her face lighting up with a grin. I looked over her shoulder.

"Not just any pass. A perfect 4.0."

"Like there was any doubt," Sam said with a snort.

They both turned to look at me.

"You next, Lyssa," Kelsey urged.

She was right. I couldn't put it off forever. And if I had to re-sit over the summer, it wouldn't be the end of the world. At least it would give me something to keep myself busy with.

Sam coughed.

"Alright, alright," I grumbled. "I'm doing it."

I pulled out my sheet of paper, flipped it over, and scanned it. In the top right-hand corner was my grade. 3.0. A pass. Not a great one, but who cared? A pass was a pass. Underneath was a breakdown of my exam results. My best was Supernatural Zoology with a near perfect score, followed closely by Elemental 101. My worst was Sepllcraft, I'd barely scraped a forty. No surprise there. And the less said about Gaelic, the better. But a pass. I'd take that any day of the week.

"She's smiling," Kelsey said. "Is that a good smile, or a bad smile?"

Sam reached over and plucked the sheet from my hands.

"Second year, here we come."

"Congratulations!" Kelsey squealed. "We did it. We all did it!"

All around us, squeals of excitement and groans of disappointment erupted, and the volume of chatter grew louder and louder until I almost had to shout to make myself heard.

"I can't believe I'm not going to see you guys for two months!"

"We'll stay in touch," Kelsey said, pulling a scrap of paper from her bag and scribbling on it. "My phone number. We'll have to get together in the summer, all of us. And we should get our books early, so we can get a head start on next year's lessons. Everyone says it's going to be much harder and we don't want to fall behind."

I rolled my eyes while she babbled happily on – there really was nothing that got Kelsey so excited as a new academic challenge.

"If we can get through next year without any attacks or zombies," I said, "that'll be good enough for me."

"Pfft," Sam objected. "Where's your sense of adventure? That was the only part of the year worth turning up for."

"Says you, who slept through most of it."

We laughed, and talked about anything and everything as we finished our last meal at Dragondale. My mind was only half on our conversation, the rest of my attention split between disbelief at the amazing turn my life had taken this year – finding out I was a druid, learning to use my magic, and discovering a whole world I'd never even known had existed – and a thrill of anxiety about what was still ahead of me. Two more years at the academy, and then who knew what I would be off doing, and where my magic would take me? I knew one thing though, as I looked left at Kelsey, and right at Sam: the friendship we'd formed would last a lifetime.

As for the rest of it? Only time would tell, but I was in no rush. For the first time in my life, I'd found the place where I was truly in my element.

A note from the author

Thanks for joining me for Lyssa's first year at the Dragondale Academy of Druidic Magic. I hope you enjoyed it as much as I did. Be sure to come back for her second year in Feral Magic, book 2 in the Druid Academy series.

Meanwhile, if you enjoyed this book, I'd be really grateful if you would take a moment to leave me a review.

Sign up to my newsletter by visiting www.cschurton.com to be kept up to date with my new releases and received exclusive content.

There's one thing I love almost as much as writing, and that's hearing from people who have read and enjoyed my books. If you've got a question or a comment about the series, you can connect with me and other like-minded people over in my readers' group at

www.facebook.com/groups/CSChurtonReaders

Printed in Great Britain
by Amazon

52746169R00163